Slave to
the Farm

erika tafel

First Class Press
Algonquin College
1385 Woodroffe Avenue,
Ottawa, ON, Canada K2G 1V8
613-727-4723 ext. 5044   613-727-7744 Fax
www.facebook.com/FirstClassPress

Copyright © 2013 by: Erika Tafel

Revision Copyright © 2015 by: Erika Tafel

Cover Design: Erika Tafel

Graphic Designer: Rayana Pedlar

Editor: Ellen Tolson

ISBN: 978-1-55323-714-3

Printed in Canada
REVISED EDITION

love & music

Dedicated to the memory
Of
Tina Poux
Christina Cain
Michelle Thibault &
Tiffany Mackenzie,
The four girls who lost their
lives in the Le Village fire on
January 19, 1990

Table Of Contents

Introduction

This book has taken me years to write, and now that it is done, I sometimes pick it up and find it hard to believe it's my story. From this vantage point it certainly feels like it happened to someone else in another lifetime. The stories that follow are remembered and re-remembered from decades ago. Time has misted my memories till the edges are no longer sharp, but there are those snapshots, so crystal clear I can still smell the smells, and taste the tastes. I guess those are a big part of why I wanted to write this book in the first place. If I remember them, then others will too.

As I went over my own stories in my head, I wondered about all the other Shawbridge kids that have passed through The Farm. Thousands of them, going all the way back to the turn of the century. Where are their stories?

I started looking and found nothing. I thought, "This can't be". There are quite possibly eighty-ninety-one-hundred-year-old former Shawbridge clients still living today, but no stories?

I went to McGill University in Montreal hoping to read everything I could about Shawbridge. McGill has supplied graduate after graduate to numerous institutions that make up the Quebec juvenile system with Shawbridge (now Batshaw) being one of its oldest juvenile placements. I was shocked when I could only find a grand total of three books about the one hundred year old institution: two of them in the rare book section printed before 1940, and the third one, I'd already read, *Normal Bad Boys, Public Policies, Institutions, and the Politics of Client Recruitment*, written by Pru Rains and Eli Teram.

How tragic that what happened to us there wasn't being preserved or documented in any way.

I didn't have a high school graduation class to identify with, so I chose to identify with Shawbridge kids and started calling them, 'Grads', adding all of us to The Farm alumni. I took interviews of all the grads I could find. I realized that despite some nail-curling stories, we all had positive stories too, many of them, in fact. We missed it in this strange way. There was this undeniable trauma bonding that had gone on among the people in each unit and all of us on The Farm. I heard more than once about this feeling of community that was present on The Farm. A feeling many grads were still trying to replace as adults.

In the end, I came to believe very strongly that it's important for stories like mine to be told. Not only because it may encourage more like it, but also because I wanted to start a dialogue that seems to be missing from the juvenile justice discussion.

There are many stories/books/articles about clients/patients/inmates in all kinds of institutions, but these stories are rarely from the client's point of view. The history most often preserved is by the policy makers, professionals, and industries that benefit from having more and more control over the lives of the people who live in these places. These histories are written by the winners, so to speak, and are lacking in the areas of human experience.

I'm hoping my book speaks to that human experience and reminds history that we were people in those institutions and not statistics, or redacted names in documents.

This book isn't warm and fuzzy, but remind yourself that I'm actually one of the lucky ones. I made it through somewhat scarred, but I found healing. Some kids aren't so lucky. Some just graduate to the adult system, pretty much believing they were destined for it all along.

Erika Tafel
November 2012

Slave to the Farm

WE DON'T NEED NO EDUCATION

We don't need no — Ed-u-ca-tion —
We don't need no — Thought control —

PINK FLOYD

I spent most of my fourteenth year locked in a 10 X 10 room. I planted many dreams for my future there. No soil to mix my hands through or seeds to lovingly care for, but plant dreams I did tirelessly. I like to think I learned a little patience waiting for those dreams to germinate, but unfortunately, I also killed many of the delicate hopefuls pulling them from their dirt womb before they were ready.

It was, however, an irreplaceable education* being locked in that room killing time instead of locked in some high school doing the same thing, and I don't use the word education lightly.

Ultimately, I believe, it was the compulsory school system* that started me down the rabbit hole in the first place.

I couldn't explain it then, but today I see schooling used primarily as a tool of social manipulation and programming. Sanctioned

5

propaganda, coupled with constant fear mongering keep children infantilized, adults economically indentured, and our culture spiritually starving to death.

My adolescent resistance really was about thought control: the control of my thoughts, and I was ready to fight to the death, but I couldn't quite verbalize to anyone why I thought I was in so much danger. I just knew they were lying to me at school and that it was a dark and scary place.

As a child, I recognized something in the school system that made me shut down inside. I just couldn't make myself endure. It wasn't until many years after being released from the juvenile system* that I even began to consider how destructive the school system had been to my life, or how it was the genesis of my placement under youth protection* in the first place. The more that came into focus, the more I recognized how destructive the education system is in all children's lives.

A study of the global education system is a head-scratcher all right. The convoluted subject can stump you just trying to define what education is. I mean it's a good thing, right?

Well, when I looked closer at it, I came to the conclusion that our children's minds are being subverted from cradle to grave and we do very little to protect them from this constant attack on their common sense. Institutions demand our children give up their time, imaginations, and inventive creativity in exchange for a lifetime of servitude and economic slavery. In fact, in many instances, we demand it.

We are endlessly 'taught' how to live our lives. Why we should give away our power, and why we should be perpetually afraid, all for our own protection. We have been deluded into believing in myths, and nowhere are these myths perpetuated more effectively than in the pavlovian boxes* we call schools. Complete with the bells and whistles to make salivating dogs out of all of us.

There is plenty of evidence to show how effective compulsory schooling is at population control. Behaviour modification techniques are studied and used on children, the elderly, the military, and of course, prisoners. Never to create a better, more compassionate world, but to control more and more aspects of it. As a culture, we don't protect ourselves from it, and certainly don't protect our children from it. We seem to accept the everyday use of physiological warfare delivered at school as a necessary evil, never really factoring in the toll it has on our collective behavior. The traditional state-sanctioned views are touted as protection against an assumed future, instead of the cause of many dysfunctions in our daily lives.

Everyday "normal" people, people who never question what or why they are doing it, most stringently police those politically correct views.

"What's rather curious is that while I firmly believe school played a major part in getting me

Slave to the Farm

into so much trouble, it also played a major role in turning me around. The coldness, cruelty, and insensitivity of so many of the teachers I encountered made me lash out in anger and frustration... I understand bitterly from many of my own experiences how teachers can wreck a kid's life." Victor Malarek- *from the book **Hey Malarek.***

My acting career started when I used to fake illness and get to stay home from school alone. I remember starting that con in grade three.

The owl's class at St Paul's Elementary in Beaconsfield was the first class I ever skipped out on. I was nine years old. That was the beginning of a long and highly successful career of academic avoidance. * I was good at it and the skills needed to master it came easy for me.

I was ill prepared, however, for an incident that happened when I was in grade six. The local Catholic priest came to offer repentance to all us sinning eleven-year-olds at St Paul's Elementary. The need to unburden our seemingly damned souls was obvious to anyone with eyes, but the only problem was, none of us knew what sins we were supposed to be confessing to.

We all knew it was bad to lie and steal, but there were so many grey areas I wasn't sure of, or how they applied to me. I had this sense that there were a lot of potential sins revolving around the ambiguous sex topic I'd heard so little about, and that there were plenty of ways to get on God's shit

8

list that way, but I didn't know any specifics. Was it considered a sin to like a boy? I wasn't sure if it was good or bad.

Filled with questions, I remember being in a state of panic, and desperate to do the right thing, I had to know what was right to have done wrong. I'm still not sure what mortal sins elementary school children are predisposed to, that would have them burning in hell for all eternity, but I remember standing there with my two closest school friends trying to think of appropriate transgressions. We stood arguing about what we would say, and jealously protected our decided upon offenses.

"You can't use that one, that's my sin!"

In the end, I don't remember what I said, but I'm pretty sure I made it up on the spot. The experience has stayed with me though, and was the glue that has stuck me with a guilty conscience ever since. Not for things I've done, but for things I don't know how to do. It's the only time I've ever been to confession that I actually remember.

Somewhere the connection was made in my brain that, to not know something is sinful, or at least something to be ashamed of. As long as I felt guilty about something, it was a pretty safe bet I was doing it right. As long as I believe I was a sinner, finding something to feel guilty about is easy. Guilt to me was like a comfort food, so feeling guilty for all the things I didn't know how to do seemed like a sure fire way to getting fat and happy.

Today I joke by calling myself a recovering

9

Slave to the Farm

Catholic who owes my salvation to a courageous older brother who refused to be confirmed in the church before me. He gave me the fuel to turn away by softening my Catholic mother. See to me, he looked like the golden boy who always did what he was told. This act of defiance was inspiring, and I secretly supported him from the invisible shadows of my younger sister status. The fact that he could not be made to concede to the ultimate salvation of his soul, paved the road for my younger brother and me to throw away our spots in heaven, too.

By the time I was twelve, I was skipping every class I could get away with and some of the ones I couldn't. I'd spend my time hanging out at Fairview Mall in Pointe Claire.

More often though, I would take the school bus from my house on Preston Drive in Beaconsfield to St Thomas High School in Pointe Claire, only to get off and rush to catch transit back to Beaconsfield. I would beeline to Beaconsfield High School, located within walking distance from my parents' house.

I attended BHS* classes with my buddies, was a regular in the smoking pit,* and was there often enough to have people think I was enrolled... teachers included.

I wanted very much to go there, but alas, it was a Protestant school, and I was to be blessed with a Catholic education. So in the spirit of making mountains out of molehills, I majored in guilt and sailed through with straight A's.

John Holt was an author and educator best known for his radical theories on schooling. *'Growing Without Schooling',* a newsletter he published regularly helped educate a nation. His efforts to protect youth's rights, and his disillusionment with the American education system, made him a pioneer in the homeschooling movement* in the 1970s.

I was introduced to his books in my mid-thirties and already a homeschooling mom of two, but what I read there set me free. His words put into context the tragedy of what had happened to my childhood. It gave me evidence, so to speak, that there was something to my unwavering resistance to the schooling system. A language opened up to me that helped me justify my views and allowed me to quit blaming my parents for not loving me enough. I learned to forgive myself for being unable to acquiesce. It gave me the validation that I did in fact recognize something in the education system that was profoundly demeaning and destructive to children, even if I was a child myself when I first noticed it.

In the end, John Holt's book *'Escape from Childhood'* convinced me that I am doing the best thing I can for my own children by homeschooling them, and that there is indeed a professional community who believed I am not hurting them, but protecting them.

Slave to the Farm

I feel I am protecting their minds from the social conditioning that's needed to perpetuate the modern myths of politics and war. The book also made it obvious to me that there is, in fact, another force that tries relentlessly to confuse and hide the truth from all of us.

Mr. Holt says *"Education... now seems to me perhaps the most authoritarian and dangerous of all the social inventions of mankind. It is the deepest foundation of the modern slave state, in which most people feel themselves to be nothing but producers, consumers, spectators, and 'fans,' driven more and more, in all parts of their lives, by greed, envy, and fear. My concern is not to improve 'education' but to do away with it, to end the ugly and anti-human business of people-shaping and to allow and help people to shape themselves."*

He describes how surprised he was once while giving a speech to a high school class, and just as he was wrapping up, he thought to ask how many of the kids in the room would live away from their parents if they were given the chance. The overwhelming majority raised their hands.

If I had been there, my hand would have flown up before anyone else's and if he had called on me for my reasons why, I would have said, "Because then I wouldn't have to go to school."

Not that I wanted to move away because I didn't love my family or because I wouldn't have a curfew, not even to avoid doing chores or going to bed when I was told, but simply because I hated school, and felt like I was wasting my time there. None of my caregivers agreed. I'm willing to bet a lot of those kids would have agreed with me, though.

Here I was, from a good home with loving parents, and still I couldn't fit into 'normal' society. Everyone around me seemed to be zombies who didn't notice they were dead. I was by no means challenged. I could do the schoolwork, but I didn't want to. I didn't see any value in it and felt like a cow in a herd of cattle. I lived in constant fear of being chosen as someone's next meal. School for me was a constant humiliation, not to my person, but to my common sense.

Lucky for me, I was one of the popular girls. I can't imagine how the kids who were not in the cool cliques made it through the day. I wasn't bullied, and was always one of the first ones picked for a team. I had friends, boyfriends and wannabe friends. I always had dates for the dances, and if I didn't, I went home with one for the next one. Looking back now, I see how very narrow my ideas were about how most of the world lives.

I knew there were poor people in the world; I just didn't know any of them. If I did, I didn't notice they were poor. I had no idea what hurdles made up their day, or that being poor meant you sometimes didn't eat. The violence, the frustration, the crime, they were only stories that I heard about on the news.

In school, I believed that the poor were poor

due to their own inadequacies, or lack of education. I ate gourmet food, and had all the creature comforts I ever wanted or needed, so I must have deserved them... right?

I vividly remember lying in my cell at Le Village* in St. Jerome Quebec, thinking about writing down what was happening to me. Even then, I believed this story had historic value. Somewhere, somehow, I knew someone would be interested. I didn't have a clue exactly what was happening myself but… shit man, I know when something feels right and when it doesn't. There was so much wrong with what was going on all around me I thought someone should pay attention, and do something.

I was locked up twenty-four hours a day for not going to school, I think? Psychologists, sociologists, psychiatrists, social workers, doctors, specialists or anyone with letters attached to their name, all studied me. They all agreed there was something wrong with me, but none could figure out what to do about it. Nobody seemed to agree with me about anything I thought would help. I felt like I was constantly being chastised about how uncooperative I was. My suggestions were always diminished and cast off as having no value. That old saying, 'Damned if you do, damned if you don't," was my comfortable conundrum.

"I could work with horses! I could go to France!"

"Erika, really, you're just too young" or

14

Slave to the Farm

"You're throwing away your future if you don't finish school." Common themes of encouragement showered down upon me from above. They described future imminent lifestyles for me: jail, homelessness, single parenting, or dying young. All unless I pulled up my bootstraps, flew straight and did what they told me to do.

"Even garbage men need a high school diploma, Erika". Nobody cared that I didn't want to be a garbage man. Nobody cared that I didn't want to be any of those things on their list of possible career choices. I never did see social or environmental activism on any of their lists.

The choices given all included high school as a 'must have' to take a step forward in this enormous board game of life, but fuck the board game. I didn't want to play, and that was just too much for the ologists* to put up with. I think that was really what they tried hardest to cure me of.

I just wanted to point out flaws; chinks in the armor of the traditional system that seemed to stack the deck against me every time, but noticing these obvious flaws as a budding teenager seemed to be viewed as rude and not worth discussing, anti-social even. I just couldn't understand how what seemed so easy for me to see was completely ignored by the powers that be, including my parents.

When I was a child, most of the adults in my life were hypocrites. Now, as an adult, I still face the same hypocrisy every day. Shut up, put up and drink yourself into submission. That seems to be the safest road to travel if you happen to notice the overwhelming injustices and insanity of this life.

Their professional predictions for my demise did not come true. I didn't get pregnant as a teen, fall sick of some sexual disease, or become a heavy drug user. I'm not homeless and destitute on the street. It isn't necessary for me to prostitute my body, or collect welfare. Believe it or not, I've even had a good job or two in my wasted high school dropout life.

I grew up to become so much more than they predicted. I'm a filmmaker, community activist, singer, teacher, event organizer, mother, wife, truth-sayer, and a colossal pain in the ass. Oh yeah, and now a writer, all this without a high school diploma.

Where does one start? I was born in La Tuque, Quebec, the second of three children and an only daughter. We moved to Montreal when I was seven. My father was an engineer, and my mother a nurse. Or, do you want to hear the juicy stuff first?

I left home for the last time at fourteen, begged, borrowed, stole to survive, found myself staring down the barrel of a shotgun more than once, hitchhiked many of North America's highways, and was raped by a distant relative's high school sweetheart.

All those experiences left residual skid marks in my life, but my stay at Shawbridge Youth Centre,* "The Farm",* was a tattoo on my sub-conscience. I rely on the eyes and ears I got there every day.

Actually, Le Village* in St- Jerome is where I did the majority of my time in the system, but The Farm was the end of the line for the kids like me.

17

Slave to the Farm

When my skipping at St. Thomas came to a head and administration could not ignore it anymore, I was caught and sent to the school guidance counselor, again. She had contacted my parents many times concerning my truancy, and on her suggestion, they contacted a social worker at Ville Marie Social Services.*

Over the next few months, my parents and I played the most robust game of Ping-Pong, knocking my compliance and defiance back and forth, but one of us finally dropped the ball. That huge hairy hairball was the ultimatum: live at home and go to school, or be placed in the system and go to school.

To me this seemed like a choice between country or western, neither of which I could stomach at the time, but everyone else seemed to think there was a huge difference between the two. Living away from home would get me away from the disappointed eyes of my family, and I thought it would be kind of like traveling, but ... I still had to GO TO SCHOOL!?

It wasn't that I didn't love my family, or want to be with them, but this very slippery slope had been developing between them and me. Because I wasn't going to school during the day, it was very hard to go home at night. I took to not coming home at all. My mother was hysterical when this would happen, and even more hysterical when I did finally saunter through the door.

Slave to the Farm

I got high, or drunk before going home, knowing what I was in for when I got there. If I was lucky, we would just fight about my level of inebriation, and avoid the ever deepening and more troubling problem of my growing depression.

Many of the kids I met at Shawbridge Youth Centre started miles behind me in the silver spoon department, and there behind those locked doors, my eyes were opened for the first time to the pain that many children face daily. Drug addicted parents, abandonment, hunger, prostitution, violence, and sexual abuse were all par for the course in many of their homes.

I thought, "What the hell am I doing here? I don't fit into the same category as these people." But I didn't fit in with my own stratum, either. If I even had a stratum. The system kids seemed to understand my resistance to authority more than any other peer group I'd ever encountered at school.

The school children were perpetually afraid of retribution, and numbed into cowardliness. The kids in the system were fearless, and willing to take many risks. I wanted to be more like them.

Our reasons for being in Shawbridge were as vast as the ocean is wide, but etched into all of our faces was an expression that said "SOMETHING IS VERY, VERY WRONG!!" We were all facing different challenges; we were all looking at the same warped picture and reacting to the violence bequeathed from generation to generation.

Slave to the Farm

The longest stint I did without running away was seven straight months at Le Village in twenty-four hour lock up. I often feel like a piece of my core is still locked up in those hallowed halls. When I close my eyes I can beam myself back there. It's like a magnet attached to my memory, pulling with all the force of the universe.

The memory is like a prison itself, never far from the surface and always seeping into my quiet moments. Although behind those locked doors, I was safe from the potential violence that comes with any life spent on the streets, I was exposed to some of the most horrific spiritual torture that my soul has ever known. Spirit-crushing humiliation.

I don't have words to describe the unquenchable need to escape the reality of my existence, if only for a few hours. I remember the weight of craving death to take me before I had to open my eyes and live another day in Skinner's box.*

A wing of the building burnt down, taking the lives of four young girls with it just three short years after I got out. I use to think it could have been me.

It all has a taste that still lingers on my tongue, reminding me of all those darker moments of doubt and self-loathing. How do you explain the humiliation you experience lining up to take medication that makes you feel sick, or being watched while you shower, or wearing communal underwear?* How do you verbalize the shame you feel because your parents visited from the suburbs every Sunday, and bring you treats, while your roommates tell stories of their addicted mothers and boyfriends turning them out* for drug money.

In the presence of those girls, I was ashamed of my privilege, my sheltered existence, and my lack of experience. I felt somehow like a fraud. I believed that I was somehow different and didn't belong among them. I couldn't really put my finger on why I was there in the first place, and neither could they.

In Le Village, I was called 'the poor little rich kid', because of the attention given to me by my family, and the entitlement that came with their visits. I was envied and resented for the same transgression. Having a dedicated family could sometimes be a liability. Who knew?

Slave to the Farm

Sweet Leaf

Black Sabbath

I smoked my first spliff * in the summer of 1981 when I was 11 years old. I was visiting my cousin Mary-Jane who was three years older. I smoked my third, fourth and fifth spliffs with her too, but it wasn't until I met Weasel the following summer that I smoked hash at home and tried acid.*

I don't remember getting high the first time, but it happened when Mary-Jane brought me over to her friend's garage and there was a group of older guys there all working on dirt bikes. They were leather wearing tough guys with wallets chained to their belts; cool dudes. I thought it was great. I'd tried cigarettes already, so when the spliff was rolled, lit, and passed around the circle to me, I just smoked it like I'd done it a hundred times before. There were a couple of people taking tokes* before me, so I just watched, learned how it was done, and then looked like an expert on my first try. I never even coughed. I thought my cousin would let the cat out of the bag that it was my first time, but she kept my dirty little secret.

Slave to the Farm

We were all lighting up smokes after the session* when one of the guys asked if I wanted to try kicking over his bike. After giving it a good hard try, and not wanting to admit defeat, I started getting tired and sloppy. My legs filled with Jell-O. After a particularly ungraceful attempt, I fell over, pulling the bike on top of me. I slammed into the line of other bikes that dominoed and fell over too. I was horrified, but everyone else burst out laughing.

When I finally untangled myself from the pile, I was so embarrassed I just wanted to go home. I had a bruised and bleeding shin with a matching ego. While nursing my wounds, everyone assured me that no harm had been done, but I was sure they all thought I was an idiot. My cousin whispered reassuringly, "Don't worry about it, they love you!" And they did. I think I got to ride on every one of those dirt bikes numerous times that summer.

By the end of the summer of 1981, I was a veteran OPS hashish smoker. OPS, meaning Other People's Supply. I never bought it, didn't know what it cost, nor did I understand how it was sold in weights. It was just generously supplied to me for free. If I spent any money on something to smoke, it was cigarettes. I practiced smoking hard that summer.

My first smoke was at five years old. I stole a pack of my mother's Craven A's and got caught out behind the garage with them. I tried it again when I was ten with a pack of Winstons in the basement, but what truly started the daily habit was finding a pack of Green Death* with my neighbour and best friend Juju.

We sat at Beaconsfield High School on that sweltering summer day in 1982, and smoked, and smoked, and smoked that pack away. By thirteen I was hooked, and smoking every day. A loyal Export 'A' customer for decades.

Juju was the first friendly face I met when I moved to Beaconsfield in 1977. She lived right next door, and was a year older. I thought she was great, and we were best friends for years. We spent many hours together before I started getting in trouble with the system.

Juju and I were starting to drift apart. Our interests began changing and diverging. Our mothers, who had been friends for years, weren't talking to each, and it put a huge strain on our relationship. I was developing an interest in boys much more quickly than she was, and experimenting with drugs, something she never dreamed of doing.

For years, our families had been sharing meals, and her mother, Auntie Elvis, was very special to me. I was able to talk to her about many things I would never dream of sharing with my own parents. I thought of her as a friend. That too was strained because I had to sneak in and out of her house to avoid irritating mom.

I had no sisters, and the topic of the birds and bees was, to my mother anyway, strictly a gardening subject, so when I started to bleed I never mentioned it to her. I don't even remember how old I was when I started my menses. There was no big celebration, no cake, and while I guess I was supposed to recognize it as a great achievement in my maturation according to the very few paragraphs I'd read on the subject, I hid it at all costs.

If every girl in my grade six class hadn't of received that little pink book entitled *"So You're A Women Now"* at school, I may not have even known what was happening to me. As it was, it took years before I realized I wasn't growing public hair. I remember thinking how stupid it was to call the hair on my vagina public. What a relief to find out it was actually just my dyslexic mistake.

The padded bricks I used for my first period had been in residence in the kids' bathroom for as long as I could remember. I never really knew if they were there for me, or for any unprepared visitor who happened to find them, but I left the box empty under the sink for many moons before I finally fessed up to my mother.

I used Auntie Elvis' supply of pads when mine ran dry at home. There were three girls in her house, all older than myself, and if Auntie E noticed someone stealing bricks from her house, she never said anything about it to me.

Finally the day came when my mother was taking orders for her grocery list. Seeing my opportunity to replenish the empty box under the sink, I, without showing any emotion or interest, suggested she buy a new box of sanitary napkins.

Slave to the Farm

"There's some under the sink in your bathroom?" She started, looking up at me with understanding dawning in her eyes. "Is it empty?"

Leaning back on my chair and looking as nonchalant as possible, I answered, "Yup, I used them all up. I need more."

"Need more what? I want some. If Erika gets some I want some too. Erika gets everything. Mom can I have some?"

Ignoring my little brother, she wrote down my request and that was the end of the conversation. Never to be revisited again, but on the plus side, the box under the sink was never empty again.

The physical needs of my brothers and I were paramount to my mother. We never lacked for anything. I had beautiful things all around me growing up, and our childhood friends often came over to my mother's kitchen because of its great food. If the gang hung out in anyone's basement, it was ours. No one understood why I didn't want to be there. Everyone loved my mom and dad. No one understood me. My loneliness and depression grew right alongside of my hormones.

I spent every moment I could with my boyfriend in the spring and summer of 1982. I was twelve. Weasel was two years older than me and I was in love. We did a lot of kissing and hand-holding, but really we spent most of our time wrestling. He would grab my knee and pinch it so hard that I had to hold back tears. He would plow

27

me into the ground head first till I was picking grass out of my teeth.

Juju and Weasel are connected indelibly in my mind because of the time she caught us, millimetres from ripping our clothes off and losing our virginity together.
She was hip to exactly what was going down there, and was having no part of it, so neither could I.

My parents were at work and it was that magical time between when I got home from school and when my mother would come home from work. It was my coveted and preciously guarded 'free time' when I didn't have to answer to anyone. It was the time when I wasn't being watched, evaluated or tested. I guess it was the time when I learned the most about my own interests good or bad, and at that particular moment my interests were purely physical.

Juju came right in, sat down on the bed, and made herself comfortable. I don't remember her saying anything to us, but the look on her face said enough. She wasn't leaving no matter what. While her concerns were of course valid, she was trying to protect the virtue and virginity of a young vulnerable girl. She did foil my choice of whom I first 'va-va-voomed!'

Ah, young love... I mention him because it was with him I started drinking on the weekends, and I was with him the first time I took acid.

His friend, Butt, had an older brother who would sometimes buy us beer at the local Provi-

Slave to the Farm

Soir*. If Bro wasn't around, we had our own ways of meeting our brewing needs, like bottle-burning, as we liked to call it.

We would walk around the neighbourhood looking for open garage doors. If beer cases were visible we would run in and steal them. If they had beer in them, we would head straight to the beach, but if they didn't, we cashed in the bottles and found someone to buy beer for us. We would head to Memorial Beach on Beaconsfield Boulevard and get drunk sitting along the black murky waters of Lake St. Louis.

Or, more accurately, he would get drunk, and I would gag back a beer...maybe.

I hate beer. Well, maybe hate is too strong a word, but I don't understand why people like the taste. None of my boyfriends have ever complained about this particular oddity, and I've always believed my dislike of beer played a big part in avoiding alcoholism as yet another skill listed on my resume.

I don't mean to suggest that I haven't been rip roaring drunk on too many occasions, but drinking was never my bag. I can handle a glow, but anything beyond that sends me face first to the 'Altar of Ass'. * Black hash, and of course cigarettes down at the beach, became my drugs of choice, until I was introduced to psychedelics.

Slave to the Farm

Psychedelics are illegal because they dissolve opinion structures, and culturally laid down models of behaviour and information processing. They open you up to the possibility that everything you know may be wrong. -Terence McKenna-

crazy train

... I'm goin' - off - the - rails - on a crazy train

Ozzy Osbourne

The first time I ran away I dyed my hair black. It was a dramatic change from my auburn hair, and a legacy to that time. I still have old friends that call me Blackie in remembrance of that asinine act. I was arrested the next day, and returned to my shocked, but thankful, parents.

I thought because I was nowhere near Memorial Beach, and I looked so different (wink, wink; nudge, nudge), they would never find me.

I was just beginning to realize that the West Island of Montreal* is not a big place. The cops just walked into the Better Dead pool hall and scooped me up. Believe me, I was learning a few other things, too, but the black-haired period in my life was the changing point in my relationship with my parents and the law.

My parents were going through a separation and my life was 'going off the rails". My father's leaving was traumatic, but I never felt like he was there very much anyway. He worked in Point-Aux-Trembles on the other side of the island, so he got up, and was gone every morning before any of us

31

were even out of bed. He came home at night just in time for dinner, and after he ate, he simply went to bed, only to get up and do it all again the next morning. Those long hours when he was 'at work', are still an enigma to me. Those hours were his other life, the one I never shared.

We got used to him not being in the house. He was never my disciplinarian, anyway. I felt like he always deferred to my mother's decisions about my upbringing, and although I missed having him around at dinner, we avoided each other mostly anyway.

I did find it much easier to communicate with my dad, though. I felt like he tried to understand me more, and had more patience for me. If I really wanted something, I would recruit him to my cause before asking my mother for permission. However, building a close relationship with my dad seemed to make my mother very angry. Getting along with my father made getting along with my mother harder. I started not coming home.

I was trying to get as far away from my feelings of failure as possible. I felt this crippling sense of hopelessness in life itself. I didn't want to be with my family, but not because I didn't care about them. I loved them deeply. I just was not able to communicate with them about how I was feeling, and being with them meant having to try. It was like trying to talk to people not merely from a different country, but from a different planet altogether.

Slave to the Farm

All my life, I've been told I think too much or not enough. They were about to put me in jail for not going to school. I didn't get a high school education, but to be fair, I did receive a university level education in behavioral studies. I learned street smarts, which is just a dumbed-down name for intuition and common sense, but incredibly valuable as a life skill on the mean streets of the suburbs. I didn't get there all at once, mind you. I was a fast learner, and luckily didn't make too many mistakes.

During the black-hair period in late 1982, I started going to a juvenile diversion program* named Madankco. The weasel, my new friend Diz, and many other West Island kids went, and spent time there dirt bike riding, jamming live music, going on organized trips, and sharing our teen-age woes with some wonderful mentors.

Papa Smurf was our group's guru, and counted as one of my friends.

Now Papa Smurf wasn't like any of the other adults I knew. For some reason I felt like I could trust him, and that he understood me. When he spoke to my parents it was from my perspective, and usually in defense of my views. I loved him. He was a six foot tall teddy bear with long shaggy hair, tattoos, and a history of jail time. What wasn't to love?

He brought us on a couple of winter camping trips. All have their good memories, like the surprise birthday party they threw me, or how funny it was when Papa Smurf ate a couple of cookies made with Ex-lax.* He had a habit of eating everyone's baked goods, so he was taught a lesson that kept him close to the outhouse and out of our personal belongings. We all got a good laugh.

On one of those camping trips, I broke my ankle. It was to become one of the most well told stories of my adolescence. I spent two weeks in the Montreal Children's Hospital because I developed a blood clot in the leg, and I had a cast from toe to hip for close to twelve weeks. I was on crutches for months after the portable sarcophagus came off.

It was the waning months of winter when we hiked across the small lake and climbed up this rock face to investigate some caves we hoped to spend the night in. After hanging out there for a little while, finding and investigating all the small caverns and starting to get bored, someone found this cliff with a ten foot drop into snow drifts up to your armpits. There were probably ten of us there, and one by one we all took our turn jumping off this rock into the snow below.

As my turn came around, I began to rethink my jump. I wasn't sure I wanted to do it anymore. I never did like heights very much, and because of being the last one to jump, the encouragement from the peanut gallery below was fierce. I felt like I would lose face among the group if I didn't at least give it a try. After all, what could happen?

"Come on, Erika, you can do it. Just like everyone else. One, two, three go." So I sucked up my bowels, closed my eyes and leaped into the void.

The sound of bones snapping was heard by everyone standing there, and the wail that escaped my lips must have sounded subhuman. The searing white hot pain that raced up my body very nearly caused me to pass out, but I managed to stay conscious. I lay there whining in the snow while everyone tried to comfort me and decide what to do next.

The cabin was several kilometres away. They dug me out of the snow, but more problematic was the fact that we had done some rock climbing to get to where we were, and that meant we also had to climb back down.

Though it had taken about a half hour to get to the cliffs, it took much, much longer to get back. I don't remember the return journey clearly, but eventually we made it to the cabin, and I was laid in bed. Everyone began to consider how to get my boots off. An attempt was made, but the pain was so agonizing the effort was abandoned, and the boot left on.

I gratefully accepted some very strong pain killers from Frenchie, whose wisdom teeth had been recently extracted. The warm glow of the opiates offered me some relief, and calmed me down, but I remained in serious distress.

Soon a plan was hatched that saw me off to the nearest hospital in St. Jerome. The first problem was the hike to where the van was parked. We normally cross country skied through the knee deep snow, or snowshoed, but I couldn't walk, or ski. I would have to be carried the whole way. A stretcher was fabbed up for that purpose, and while I faded in and out of coherency the rest of the group struggled to lug my dead weight through the snow.

It was a long and arduous process and when we got to the van, I was writhing in pain from being jostled. The people who helped carry me collapsed exhausted. After loading me into the van, most stayed behind. Papa Smurf drove while Diz and the Weasel came with me for moral support.

It was still another hour to the hospital, but we made it in record time, and I was fast tracked through the emergency ward. The hospital x-rayed my foot through the boot, and decided that the break was too severe for them to handle. I would probably need surgery, so they sawed off the boot, secured my foot in a plastic cast, and sent us on to the Children's Hospital in Montreal, another hour and a half away.

The Children's Hospital was ready for me when we got there, and after a shot of Demerol, and a new round of x-rays, we were informed that there was a problem with any potential treatment. My parents couldn't be located. The surgery that was needed could not go ahead without their consent. Papa Smurf could not sign, so the hospital couldn't operate. It was Saturday night, and my parents weren't expected to pick me up until about 8 pm the following evening. We were at a standstill.

Slave to the Farm

At the hospital I was being fed a steady stream of pain killers, and my foot didn't appear to be getting any worse, but my ankle needed to be surgically pinned. After hours of waiting for something to happen, a nurse came and told me a doctor was going to set my ankle the old fashion way... painfully.

She was there to bring me to the casting clinic to set my leg in a cast. I was told that an orthopedic specialist from out of country who was visiting the hospital agreed to set the break.

I left my body while that doctor set my mangled ankle. I don't remember any pain, but I do remember it seemed to take a very long time to get the job done. She ground, and yanked, and mashed, and jerked my ankle around while I floated somewhere near the ceiling watching dispassionately like it was happening to someone else. I watched as at last the doctor released the newly set foot from her torturous grip and the girl immediately calmed and started crying. Before I knew it was happening, I was back in my body again, and feeling all the pain following the brutal manipulation of my ankle. I hardly noticed when the nurse began wrapping my whole leg in cotton, and really didn't grasp the fact that I was getting a full leg cast till the plaster was drying.

When the casting was done, and I had a look, it didn't look like my leg at all. My foot was set at this strange pigeon-toed angle with my toes pointing straight down and my knee slightly bent into the most unnatural looking shape. Standing on my right leg, and letting the cast hang, my baby toe would have been the first thing to touch the ground. I wouldn't be able to walk on this casted leg at all, and would have crutches as long as I was in it.

I was in such pain that I couldn't sit still, and just withered away in my bed. Almost immediately, I started running a fever and the nurses became concerned about my blood pressure. The hospital decided to keep me overnight, and Papa Smurf and the gang finally left, facing the long drive back to camp.

Despite being heavily medicated, I was still in excruciating pain. I felt like my leg was burning with infection, but the nurses kept telling me I was all right, and that it would get better soon. I didn't sleep all night, and groaned and begged for more pain killers throughout the next day. I was waiting impatiently for my parents to come and collect me.

When my mother finally did come, I was so happy to see her that I started crying, and shocked her with my need of her. It had been very strained between us for many months, and she was happy to have her needy-little-girl back instead of the shit-ass-know-it-all teen she expected to pick up. She oozed sympathy and compassion, and I lapped it up like a hungry pup.

She was concerned about my condition, and questioned the medical staff on the wisdom of taking me home yet. I was still in constant and obvious pain, and even the tiniest jarring of my leg sent waves of nausea and searing pain through my entire body, but they assured us there was nothing else that could be done for me, so we went home.

By evening, I was delirious with fever, and so weak I couldn't get out of bed to go to the washroom myself. The pain was unbearable and I began to hallucinate. My mother thought it was time to bring me back to the hospital. She rushed me back to the Children's, and I was admitted and brought to a room where they intended to cut open my cast and look at my leg. They didn't want to disturb the setting of the bones, so they planned two cuts along the top of my cast, one from my big toe to my inner thigh and the other from my baby toe to my hip; then they could lift the strip of plaster off and voilà.

Easier said than done. As they began the first cut, I started to scream bloody murder. It felt like they were cutting directly into the skin of my leg. Part of the problem was the vibration from the saw. It was jarring my foot, and causing me intolerable pain, but I swore they were cutting my flesh as well. I kept screaming at the technician that he was torturing my leg, but I didn't get much sympathy until the plaster was taken off.

My leg exploded out of the constraining cast, bulging blue and yellow, and black the whole length. The relief from the strangling effect of the cast was immediate, and then the waves of pain returned.

Slave to the Farm

The medical staff was amazed, and finally sympathetic that I had managed to last as long as I did with the circulation to my leg being cut off. Tests were ordered, and I was admitted for an extended stay. I was given a bed in the orthopedic ward next to a window overlooking the Montreal Forum.*

There are many interesting stories that happened in the two weeks I spent in hospital, like dropping LSD*, or the story of the most memorable shit of my life, always good for a laugh, but the most scandalous memory was smoking.

In 1983 at thirteen, I was allowed to smoke inside the Montreal Children's Hospital. I was bedridden, so the nurses would roll my bed, IV and all, down to the elevators where the public was permitted to smoke, and I would spend most of my day there watching people come and go, all while lounging in nicotine heaven.

I had the cast removed in the spring, but my mobility was still limited for many weeks. I continued needing crutches, or I walked with a severe limp, refusing to use a cane. I still managed to skip school, and hang out at BHS every chance I got.

I got very skilled at keeping up despite my crutches, but because of my disability, I went home every night with aching arm pits.

On one of those nights in late April while my mother was working late, I called her to ask permission to go to Ozzy Osborne's *"Bark At The Moon"* concert at the Montreal Forum.

Of course she said no! She always said no. Eventually, I would just stop asking, but on that evening I begged and pleaded to get the OK. She wouldn't budge. She even threatened to have the police come and arrest me if I went out before she got home. I got a good laugh out of that one. Just another idle threat, and probably how I justified my right to go. I told her, "Tell them to look for a long-haired young girl, wearing a leather jacket and blue jeans just outside The Forum."

They couldn't miss me among the throngs of other long haired, leather-wearing young girls out that night.

I met up with my friends downtown, dropped acid, and never once worried about my mom, or the police.

Diz and I had been developing a friendship that included many acid trips. We shared many hours of altered states together. Although she was my acid partner, I often felt more like a travel guide. Diz would sometimes bad trip,* and I would spend much of my energy trying to calm her down. She would whip herself into a froth until she bubbled over, and would take off leaving me to either chase her, or stress about her whereabouts for hours before I would speak to her again. She would call, say she was sorry, and then tell me all about her trip without me.

41

Slave to the Farm

I was hoping that night would turn out differently. My doubts grew as Diz visibly wound up tighter and tighter next to me.

As we were trying to make ourselves comfortable and finding space for my crutches, Diz started to really peak*. Luckily, the two French guys smoking primo black hash in front of us, were more than happy to let me elevate my foot between their chairs, and smoke us on their gold stamp.* It calmed her down a bit, but even with the lights still on, Diz started the predictable banter that told me she was heading for a crash.

I tried to calm her, and get her excited about seeing Ozzy. She seemed to calm down when the French guys lent us binoculars to scan the crowd seated around us. We located, and watched a speckling of our friends, but when the lights went out she struggled through the opening band.

I tried to convince her to calm down, and said everything would be alright. Diz tried hard, but was losing the battle. Her anxiety was rising with every energy-driven song.

It got better briefly during intermission, but by the time Ozzy came on stage, Diz was peaking again. I was so into seeing the concert that I started watching the stage on my right more and more, while she built up pressure on my left. She kept screaming in my ear that she wanted to leave, but I begged her not to. We could barely hear each other over the amplified rock'n'roll. Leaving for me meant crawling over many people dragging my leg behind

42

me and then wandering around downtown on crutches with aching arm pits. Besides, this was Ozzy... you don't just get up and walk out on Ozzy!

But that is exactly what she did during a smoking guitar solo that had me head-banging to Suicide Solution. I turned just in time to see her break through into the aisle, and bound down the steps that took her to the exit.

A moment of panic froze my heart. Should I go after her? I never could have caught her being the gimp that I was, so I just sat there feeling sorry for myself. The pulsing music kept drawing my attention back to the stage, and when the French guy's next spliff came around, I was resolved to the fact that there was nothing I could do till the concert was over. I sat in my altered state and experienced Ozzy alone.

When the fat lady had sung her last song and the lights came up, I realized with mounting dread that my crutches were missing. Sometime during the concert they had been pinched. Everyone around me was leaving. The French guys invited me to go with them, but I sat there too embarrassed and shell-shocked to ask them for help, so said no thanks.

All my potential knights in shining armour were heading quickly towards the exits, and I think I was mere inches from hysterical tears when I spied someone I knew.

I was so happy to see him, I thought he glowed with an inner light, and stood out as somehow different from everyone around him. It

43

was like in the movies when the main character enters a really dramatic scene with the music crescendo in the background.

He had all the necessary armour required of a hero: the leather, the hair, and a strong enough back to carry me home.

"Gimli brother, you gotta help me!" I screamed out from the middle of an empty row of stadium seats.

He was surprised to see me sitting there alone, and came over. I told him all about Diz bad-tripping on the acid, and about the missing crutches, and begged him to help me get home. I was not a very big girl, but Gimli was not all that big himself. Good thing he was built like a brick shit house, and he made a fine warrior in my eyes. With a lot of effort that was not at all graceful, I climbed onto my steed, and off we rode to Atwater metro station.

Now, as you can probably guess, I was in no rush to face my extremely pissed-off mother, so I was happy to sit in Windermere Park, a few blocks from my house, and polish off the jar of jungle juice* that Gimli had jammed in his jacket. I was coming down off the acid and getting very drunk off the different liquors in Gimli's juice. So was he. It was sometime after 3 a.m. when I finally got to my doorstep, and watched Gimli stagger off into the sunrise.

I met my mother's pink slippers at the top of the stairs as I inch-wormed my way up. She must have watched me crawling up the stairs and wished she could just push me right back down them.

"Where are your crutches?" was all she could manage to croak out when I reached the top.

"I lost them at the concert." I sheepishly whispered.

"Well it's a good thing you won't be needing them, you're grounded! Jesus Christ, what am I going to do with you? Look at you. You're drunk. Why, Erika? Why do you do this to me? Do I deserve this?" The hurt and disappointment pooling in her eyes was like alcohol on an open wound.

I really didn't want to hurt her, but I never felt like we played for the same team. I felt like nothing I did ever pleased her, and that my interests were better kept to myself. Nothing I ever wanted was judged realistic, or worthy of pursuit. I don't know how or when we became adversaries, but there in those teenage shoes I felt like we were head to head in some to-the-death competition. Never really knowing what we were competing for.

"Well... don't you have anything to say?"

"I don't know" my standard answer for everything.

"Get to bed and we'll discuss this in the morning."

The economic necessity of feeding a family dragged my mother to work the next morning before I even crawled out of bed. I limped around until new crutches were re-supplied, but the reality of policing a punished teenager, even with a broken leg, made the blip that was Ozzy pass quicker than I could have hoped.

As a parent, I now understand how much energy goes into making sure that your standing orders are followed, and years of trying to get my own children to do as I say have taught me that you can't make anyone do what you want them to... ever! I've learned to never threaten a consequence I wasn't ready or able to enforce with full and total commitment, because anything less just proves to your children that you are full of shit.

At that time, I had no understanding of the stress that working adults were under to support growing families, or how many different issues pulled at them, and demanded their full and undivided attention.

I resented the fact that my parents were always at work, but I also saw that demand as a godsend, affording me the free time I so craved.

Ridiculously, I believed that adults were free to do what they wanted, whenever they wanted to do it. I didn't believe my parents when they told us how much they would rather stay home with us. I didn't recognize that they were as much slaves and indentured servants in our social myth as I felt I was.

Over The Hills And Far Away

Many times I've loved   Many times been bitten

Many times I've gazed a- long the open road—

Led Zeppelin

Lachine Shelter was my first placement. I met some of the kids that I would know for at least three more years on the treadmill known as Ville Marie Social Services there. My roommate was also a first timer. Lollipop arrived the same Saturday that I did. She seemed so young and naïve even to me, a greenhorn* myself. I still remember her wearing those hot pink corduroys and a striped pink and white shirt.

She was kind of nerdy looking with greasy long straight black hair and thick glasses. Her dark skin intrigued me. I wondered where her accent was from. My elementary and high schools were filled with white-middle-class-catholic children, maybe with the occasional coloured kid mixed in, but I had never spent much time with such an ethnic looking and sounding girl before, or at least one I could talk to.

Slave to the Farm

She had arrived a few hours before me, and had already settled into what was to be our room. She was on her bed reading when we were introduced.

At first, our conversation was strained, neither of us really knowing what standard operating procedures were when meeting another internee, but by the time dinner was called we had become the type of best friends proximity creates.

We sat together at dinner and underwent the inspection that happens every time a new kid was introduced into a group placement.

I remember being very uncomfortable and shy around the other kids. I was sure they wouldn't like me, and I would never fit in. I was very thankful to have Lollipop there with me to help carry the weight of all those staring eyes. It was a relief when we finally retired to our rooms.

Lollipop and I talked long into the night about our families and friends. Mostly we talked about our boyfriends. The topic we avoided at all costs was why we found ourselves in the situation we were in.

I had already decided that I was going to run when they let me out to go to school, but I never brought that up to Lollipop.

On the following day, the kids living at the shelter had plans to go to the movies, and they left as a group not long after breakfast. Because Lollipop and I were new, we weren't allowed to go with them. We spent the day watching TV or some other mind-numbing activity until everyone returned. A few new kids returning from their weekend privileges also filed in.

We ate dinner, and I heard every agonizing second tick away till I could get to my bed. I couldn't sleep when I finally got there, and spent most of the night dreaming about getting away the following day.

Lachine Shelter* was an open unit, which meant that we weren't locked into our rooms at night and during the day all the kids went to their own schools on public transportation. The longer you were in the shelter the more privileges you were granted, like weekends at home with your family or being able to go to the mall and hang out, but I would never stay long enough to gain any of those privileges.

When Monday morning dawned, Lollipop was up and ready before I even cracked open my eyes. She had her bed made and was dressed in the pink outfit she had donned the day we met. Her excitement was obvious and I asked her what all the good cheer was about. She admitted that she didn't plan on coming back after school, and in fact, was going to New York City with a family friend. I laughed and told her I wasn't planning on returning either. We found that hilarious. We wondered what the night would be like when neither of us came home.

Slave to the Farm

At breakfast we were given two bus tickets to get to and from school, and then off we went in opposite directions.

I never even showed up at ST. Thomas High School that morning. Instead, I took the city bus to BHS. I got there after the first morning bell, and had to wait until recess before anyone I knew showed up in the smoking pit. We all hung out, smoking our cigarettes until the crowd had to go back to class, and then I walked over to my parents' house and broke in. I ate a large meal and no doubt left the mess behind.

The day I walked away from Lachine Shelter with no intentions of returning was not my first attempt at running away. I'd already been AWOL* the night I dyed my hair, and there were numerous other times that I didn't come home at night.

In fact, I ran as far as Sudbury, Ontario, eight hours west of Montreal. I went to see my cousin MaryJane.

She was barely sixteen and pregnant. My mother, believing that I could somehow become infected through the phone line with teenage pregnancy, forbade me to even speak to her. I ached to talk to her in person and hear for myself how she was doing.

She had already made the decision to place her baby up for adoption, and I was in awe of her selfless act. I had barely begun bleeding myself, and understood the mechanics even less. She was my 'go-to-girl' for all things feminine, whether she was qualified for the position or not.

I felt a great loss. My life was spinning out of control, and she was the closest thing I had to a sister, so I convinced myself that she needed me. I hatched a plan to hitch-hike from Montreal to Sudbury.

I talked about it at Memorial Beach in Beaconsfield, and even did some fundraising for my trip. I also enlisted a traveling partner who insisted we take a train. I didn't know her well, she was a friend of a friend, but she was willing to go ASAP, and had enough money for both us... if I gave her the little I had.

Another bonus was that she was a few years older than I was, and looked even older than that. She could buy the tickets and get us through any of the obstacles that might suggest my needing a guardian.

Together we took the bus downtown to the VIA station, and bought two one-way tickets. I wish I could say that the train ride was long and uneventful, but something happened on that train that softened me for even bigger fish only a few months later.

It was September 1983, and while my traveling partner slept fitfully in her coach seat, a man approached me. He sat down across the aisle and struck up a conversation. I guessed him to be in his mid to late twenties, and I thought he was very good looking.

Slave to the Farm

He told me he was going out to Vancouver and asked if I had ever heard of the Headpins before. I hadn't. He told me his name was Bernie, and that he was the drummer for the band. I didn't believe him even though he looked like someone who could be in a rock band. He had long dark blond hair and faded tight fitting blue jeans, but it just sounded like a pick-up line to me. I just said, "cool".

He invited me to come and sit with him, so I moved over to his side, and we chatted away. I was really excited by his attention, and probably told him all about running away, and going to see my pregnant cousin. He seemed impressed and never mentioned how young I was.

After talking for quite a while, he asked if I wanted to go up to the observation deck. It was the middle of the night, and everyone in the car was sleeping or trying to, so I said sure.

He took my hand, led me up some stairs to the bubble car, and we took a couple of seats in the middle of the empty car.

On the way there, I ignored all the bells and whistles going off in my head, but wasn't sure how to get out of the situation I'd found myself in. I wasn't even sure I was in a situation. Actually as soon as he took my hand, I started to feel what a sacrificial lamb must as it's being led away from the herd.

As soon as we were seated, he started to kiss me. I resisted at first, but he was gentle, and kept whispering in my ear how beautiful I was, and that he loved the smell of my hair.

His sweet talk started to get more serious, and before I knew it he was telling me how much I turned him on. I wasn't sure what to think, and I certainly didn't know what I was doing to turn him on, so I thought it safest to continue to say nothing at all, looking like a doe caught in the headlights of an oncoming semi.

He took my hand, and started using it to rub his crotch. His breathing changed dramatically and he starts swearing.

"Oh yea, that's good, oooh FUCK that's good. Rub it hard baby. Oooh FUCK yea." I almost felt like I wasn't there anymore, or like my hand wasn't attached to the body. He wasn't really looking at me anymore just concentrating on the bulge in his pants, and using my hand as a means to an end.

I tried to pull my hand away, but he got more forceful and abusive in his language so I stopped resisting. He had my wrist with one hand, and worked at his zipper with the other. Before he could get his penis out though, one of the VIA employees came up the stairs and looked suspiciously at us.

"Everything alright up here?" he asked.

I knew it was my chance to get away. All I had to do was get up while the employee was standing there, but Bernie just said something about wanting to watch the stars with his girlfriend. After looking at me for conformation the night-man just nodded at us, and went away taking the opportunity to save myself with him.

Once we were alone again, Bernie freed his pecker, and looked at me with hooded eyes.

"You are going to suck my cock and if you bite me, I'm going to kill you. Do you understand?"

I just sat stunned not moving, so he grabbed my chin to look deep into my face, and asked again if I understood. I nodded, and he let go of my face with a flick of his wrist.

I took his penis in my mouth, and tried not to gag. He just kept holding my head down trying to stick it in my mouth as far as he could. He was pumping for all he was worth, all the while whispering obscenities, when suddenly he stopped pushing on the back of my head. I wasn't quite sure what was happening till he started cumming in my mouth. I was horrified, and pulled away from him in mid organism. He grabbed the back of my head emptying himself on my face, and hair. He finally let go of me, and I started to cry. He immediately stood up, and walked off of the observation deck, leaving me there like a used up rag.

I didn't know what to do. I sat trying to wipe the bleachy-smelling mess off, gagging and crying. I had to lean over to puke on the floor in between the seats, and finally when I felt ready enough, I went to find the washroom. I never laid eyes on him again.

Slave to the Farm

When I finally made it back to my seat, my traveling partner was still sleeping. I just sat there stunned trying not to feel anything. I kept asking myself why I let that happen, why I hadn't said something when I had the chance.

Despite some experience dry humping with the Weasel, I still had never seen or held a penis, and I was disgusted to my core with the idea of doing it 'willingly'.
What Weasel and I did was fun and exciting, but he had never gone beyond rubbing up against me, and at that moment I vowed no one would ever do that again.

I spent a week or two in Sudbury, but I don't have many memories about what happened in that time. I was very glad to be with Mary-Jane, that much I know. I felt safe there with my favourite aunt and uncle, but I knew my time was limited.

I was recovering from the train trip, but never said anything about it to anyone, not even Mary-Jane. The only really vivid memory I have was eavesdropping on my aunt while she spoke to my mother on the phone.

I remember Aunt Frog Eyes pleading with my mom to let me stay with them, but my mother would have none of it. I remember my Aunt saying "please, just let me try and get her through high school." But my mother wanted me put on the first plane home.

It was my first plane ride ever, and the only person I had to share it with was a sheriff sitting next to me. We didn't say a word to each other, and when the plane landed, I don't even remember if my family was there to meet me, but I was whisked away in a grey van to the first placement that saw me locked into a room overnight.

L'Escale is a juvenile holding centre for kids waiting to be picked up for transport to another placement, and a court house for juveniles. It is on Rue de Bellechasse downtown Montreal and it was the most industrial room I would ever be in.

A stainless room with a bed platform moulded into the wall. Nothing else, just the bed. I only spent one night at a time there.

I didn't actually ever go to court there, but it became the token overnight stay before a grey van came to transport me to my next placement early the next morning.

Somewhere the decision was made to place me in another group home in Kirkland. A residential house close to my parents named Amcal.* It was another open unit, and I managed to keep from running away for a couple of weeks. I think there were only six or seven of us there, and I remember liking it. It was close to my parents' house and I didn't feel like it was an institution.

The days just bled into each other. I was attending school, and was actually going to classes, but a lot had changed there. Maybe what had changed was me, but I began to feel like I had nothing in common with the kids there.

Slave to the Farm

Even my friends seemed like strangers to me. I took on this pulp fiction quality, and people started to avoid me, and talked about my 'troubles'. They suddenly grew quiet when I came around. I became lonely at school for the first time.

I still had friends in my classes, but my weeks away left me out of the loop. I couldn't 'come over' to anyone's house, because I didn't have privileges at Amcal.

After my trip to Sudbury, I felt different, like I had a very big secret to keep, despite feeling like the whole thing was written across my forehead. I became angry and short tempered. I lost the ability to relate to my friends. I felt abandoned by them. I felt like I was all alone and that no one could understand. I thought about running away all the time.

While my grade eight peers were thinking about each other I was feeling more and more suicidal. The kids at school didn't understand why I didn't just go home. They all agreed school was a drag but… "Erika; really?"

I couldn't explain it to them either. I'm sitting here now, and I can't really explain or express fully why I felt that my home life was so oppressive. I felt ashamed of everything I did there. I felt unloved and like I didn't belong, and most acutely that I wasn't good enough. I felt uncomfortable all the time; I didn't know how to make myself feel better.

Slave to the Farm

I suffered from crushing migraines and had a case of shingles when I was only thirteen: extremely painful seeping boils running from the small of my back to behind my knee.

My mother brought me to this old decaying doctor, and I still remember his face when I gingerly peeled down my pants to show him the worst case he'd ever seen. He told us it was stress related, and then asked what I had to be so stressed about?

I healed from herpes-zoster*, and moved on to burrowing an ulcer into my stomach by the time I was sixteen.

Eventually, I ran from Amcal, too, when my buddy Free Bird helped break me out one night.

Here For A Good Time

Trooper

The first time I went to Le Village, I didn't know what to expect. The grey van picked me up at L'Escale and transported me north off the island to St. Jerome. It was late afternoon when I got there.

First, I was brought to an office where all my personal belongings were catalogued and then packed away. They asked me general questions about myself: did I have allergies, did I take medication, did I smoke, was I sexually active? Then they led me upstairs to a shower room. I was asked to strip while a nurse watched, and inspected me for what I thought was evidence of drug or physical abuse. They took my clothes away, and left me standing naked.

I was then directed to take a shower with the soap and lice shampoo they provided, and afterwards I was given underwear and a long night shirt to wear. Finally, I was left alone in the first room along a long hallway.

The room was small, maybe 6' x 10' with a single bed attached to the left wall. There was a large window reinforced with a wire screen pressed between layers of glass streaming light in from outside, but I was unable to see through it.

Other than a blanket, sheets, and pillow on the bed, there was nothing in the room. I lay down and started to cry. I could hear the other girls downstairs getting ready for dinner, and wondered where they were when I was brought in.

After what seemed like an eternity, I heard someone coming up the stairs towards my door. The key hit the lock, and the sound was imprinted in my brain. Even today there is something about a lock turning open that sends a rush of relief through me. I don't like locked doors and rarely lock my own.

The staff member who had handled my intake downstairs pushed open the door, and smiled at me. He asked "Are you hungry?"

I was more interested in my first view of the inmate standing behind him than food, so I simply nodded, and stared while the girl stared back. They left a tray of food and locked the door again.

I jumped at the door to catch a glimpse of them through the small window, as they retreated down the stairs.

All I could see once they were gone was the doorway that led to the stairway and a cream-coloured cinder block wall. I ate my dinner of Shepherd's Pie, then laid down to sleep. I must have dozed off, but when the girls came up for bed they all had to march right past my little window, and I stood watching them. They all in turn looked at me staring out of my cell, but I didn't recognize any of them.

I spent the next three days in that tiny cubicle, leaving it only to use the washroom. It was a difficult three days, and I spent most of my time trying to sleep away the hours. The waking moments were filled to the brim with feelings of self-pity along with a peppering of rage at everything I could toss any blame at.

I could hear all the goings on downstairs, and couldn't decide if I wanted to be part of them or not. I obsessively watched them as they were marched past my window morning and night, and I longed for someone to talk to.

On the fourth morning, all the girls had filed passed my window and headed down for their breakfasts. I ate mine alone in my room, but finally I was brought downstairs to meet the rest of the girls.

They weren't what I expected. I thought I would be introduced to a bunch of violent, sullen, tattooed dikes, but they just looked like normal kids to me.

We ranged in age between thirteen and seventeen and there was about twelve of us in all. I could have gone to school with any of them. The cliques were obvious even on our first meeting, and I wondered where I would fit in.

It was smoke time so all the girls sat in the common room while we were given the choice of Export A, du Maurier, or Players as our preferred poison, and a single lighter made the rounds to light our first of six that day.

We all sat in the blue smoky haze of twelve burning cigarettes, and it being my first in a number of days, I tried not to puke.

I wouldn't say there was a warm fuzzy feeling of acceptance percolating among the girls, more like a relief from the boredom of many days routinely strung together with little or no change.

My new face offered something new to think and talk about, but no one seemed to include me in their conversations. I sat there as if sitting on a bed of nails, and tried unconvincingly to look nonchalant.

Finally, one of the girls threw caution to the wind and moved over beside me. She was obviously not one of the more popular girls.

I wasn't surprised when the first thing she said to me was, "These girls are a bunch of bitches".

In the early 80's, most of the 'other' girls were preppy, listening to the dance music that would eventually morph into hip-hop, rap, and the whole rave scene.

I was categorized as a woody, listening to classic rock'n'roll, wearing tie-dyes, and lamenting about how I was born a generation too late to experience the hippie scene. My friends back home sometimes called me Flower Child because of my perpetual bare feet and long flowing Indian skirts.

Lizard, my new-found friend, fit into neither of those categories. She was a punker. She had a shaved head and a blond Mohawk that stood inches off her head. We became inseparable. She sang like an angel, and we spent considerable time in those first months writing songs that we would sing together for the other girls.

We played hours of cards together, most notably the never-ending rummy game that saw scores into the tens of thousands. She really helped me make it through those first days. She also coined a nickname I still sport lifetimes later: Rica.

After that first morning smoke, we usually did school work. A woman came into the unit and I was introduced to our teacher, Tee.

I liked her at first, mostly because she often wore a bandana on her head, and I thought it made her look like a hippie. She had one on that first morning, and I thought I could learn to trust her.

All the girls just went to work on whatever subjects they had already been working on, and Tee took me aside to let me know that I would be doing a test so she could determine what level I was at.

I sat at the kitchen table filling in my test answers while the rest of the girls worked and chatted amicably in the classroom next to the common room.

I had an hour to do the test, but sailed through it in less than twenty minutes. It was well below my level, and I had no trouble with the material.

Slave to the Farm

Tee marked the paper as soon as I was finished, but I already knew I'd aced it. Tee must have thought that some of the other girls needed more help than me, because she just told me to choose a book, read it, and then write a report on it.

I sauntered over to the book case and searched the spines of the numerous books there. I found one I thought worth reading, pulled out *Go ask Alice,* and took it to the common room.

I wasn't a big reader before being locked up. I had been labeled dyslexic in grade school, helping me doubt my reading and writing abilities, but I have still managed to develop a love of the written word, despite my slow start. I ingest hundreds of books, and I still have a morbid fascination with true crime novels which was seeded right there in Le Village's common room.

I receive a mark of 99.9% on that first book report submitted to Tee. I was more than disappointed with the mark. I felt robbed of that one tenth of a percentage, and complained to Tee about it, to which she said, "Nothing in this world is perfect and can't be improved". Validating the gnawing feeling eating away at my adolescent self-esteem that I could never do anything right.

At first sight, she looked like someone I could like, but that statement left me silently screaming, "Kiss my peace sign, you cow!" I never again worked as hard to please her.

The days just blended into each other as the routine of institutional life became comfortable and predictable. I dreamed of being out on the streets again, but for the first time, I was learning to live in a small community and oddly...liked it.

My family came every Sunday, brought me snacks and cigarettes, and even more important a break in the reality that is incarceration.

Not all the girls had dedicated parents who came to visit them, and a silent resentment boiled under the surface towards those of us who did. Even some of the staff resented you for having a consistent family.

He was tall, blond, and skinny. He chained smoked, and was loud, and boisterous. To me he looked like a scarecrow. He never liked me and wasn't all that worried if I noticed or not. Most of the girls placed with me loved him madly. Lizard and I weren't among them.

In the daily routine that was Le Village, those six cigarettes were the highlight of every day and the most profound threat or treat that any staff could dangle in front of you. At least it was for me. I can think of only one girl who didn't smoke while I was there.

The Scarecrow was very fond of cutting my cigarettes for the smallest of infractions. I'm sure he enjoyed watching me squirm like a worm on a hook, while the other girls all had their smokes.

He was very generous with extra cigarettes to the gaggle of teen-age girls who nauseatingly hung on his every word. I loathed the days he was on shift. He was the one who started calling me the

Slave to the Farm

'poor little rich kid', and often justified not granting
me the extra cigarettes during the week because my
parents came every Sunday.

I'd felt humiliation at his hands many times,
but there's one experience I can never completely
wipe clean from my memory, and I wasn't even the
target of his scorn.

It had been a particularly hard day, as
sometimes happens when small groups of people
are forced to spend every waking hour together. As
supper prep was under way, the tension in the air
was choking. The Scarecrow, having had enough of
our petty bickering, cut the group's after-dinner
cigarette.

This incited near mutiny. Squaw blew up
into a full-fledged temper tantrum, throwing herself
on the floor screaming profanities at him.

These scenes did happen from time to time,
but more often than not, the days passed
uneventfully. Whenever a girl did explode into a fit
of fury, the rest of us would just be herded into the
common room to wait out the storm.

After a lot of screaming, and threats of room
programs,* Squaw was manhandled out of the unit,
and into the QR or Quiet Room. It was in a hall
outside our unit, in another part of the building. I'd
never seen the rooms or been in them.

These QRs were out of hearing range so
after the adrenalin rush calmed itself, and our
collective attitude regained its composure, we went
to the table, and ate a silent dinner.

66

Slave to the Farm

Having been cut our after dinner smoke, we went about our after dinner chores with the appropriate lackluster motivation, and then to the common room for cards.

The Scarecrow had by this time returned to the unit and was stressing us all out, pacing back and forth, looking like he wanted to say something. I just tried to become smaller, and avoided looking at him. Finally he retreated to the office.

After a hand or two of rummy he called me into the office and told me to make up a plate for Squaw. I piled it high with the leftovers from dinner, and put it all on a tray with a glass of milk. He told me to follow him, and led me out of the unit into the hall of QR cells.

I was filled with anxiety, and confused. Why would he ask me to follow him here to deliver the tray? He never chose me for anything.

We came to a door, which he unlocked and pushed open. He never really looked into the room, just stood aside to let me enter.

The rumpled blood-spattered sheets on the bed were the first thing I noticed. Time slowed down. I swung my gaze to the right. There in the corner of the room, Squaw was squatting covered in oozing lacerations, blood and feces.

She lunged at me like a cat, knocking the food tray from my hands as I backed into the Scarecrow trying to get away from her and out of that room as quickly as possible. He just pushed past me, and screamed at me to get into the hall. I backed away from the doorway like it was the gates of hell, and dropped into a ball on the hallway floor.

All I could think of was what I had seen in that room. She had looked demented and possessed. It looked like she had scraped her bloody face along the entire length of one wall. Her clothes were ripped and she had scratches on every exposed piece of skin she could reach. She had torn out her own hair and clumps were thrown around the room. She had shit and pissed on the floor and had smeared herself and the walls with it. I just lay there in shock, not really hearing what was going on, until another staff member dragged me away.

The girls in the unit had gone to the gym to play volleyball, and when asked if I wanted to join them, I begged to just be locked in my room.

I didn't have a roommate at the time, and was so thankful I wouldn't have to face anyone later to answer questions.

The next morning as that key hit the lock on my door, I was a changed person. I didn't even tell Lizard what happened. Instead, I lied about not feeling well the night before.

I've never seen or heard word of Squaw again; she was transported to another placement without returning to our unit, but she stays with me in the deep recesses of my memory. Her face is often invoked in my mind's eye as the face of frustration. My frustration and where it can lead if left unchecked.

Slave to the Farm

The thing I loved most about Le Village was playing volleyball. There was a small gym that we shared with a French juvenile boy's unit, housed on the other side of the building.

We never saw the boys that shared this gym with us, but thought about them a lot while we spent many hours blowing off steam in that space. Sometimes when you were in the washroom you could hear them using the gym, and they must have listened to us playing countless volleyball games too.

Springfield boy's cottage from Shawbridge Youth Centre came to play volleyball with us in that gym once while I was there.

The girls were so psyched. We primped and preened and readied ourselves for the big game, chewing our nails waiting for the boys to get there.

I'd never been to "The Farm", and wondered what it was like. What would the guys look like? Normal, it turned out.

We had dinner, played hard at sports and even had some time to socialize. The time passed at lightning speed and then the blip that was our co-ed gathering was over.

Soon after that night, I was introduced to something I loved even more than playing volleyball in the gym: receiving mail from the boys on The Farm.

Lancelot from The Farm was the first person to write me a letter in Le Village. It was sweet, and full of professed love for me.

Slave to the Farm

I couldn't even remember which of the ten guys he was, but I wrote him back faithfully every time I got mail.

He was mere weeks from being released, and despite promising to write me when he got out, no more love letters made it my way after he was gone. The weight of that loss was crushing. I had come to depend on those weekly letters, like a drug keeping me alive. The depression that followed was devastating. I started reading more and more.

My favourite staff was an Italian gentleman who seemed to try very hard to make up for Scarecrow's insensitive treatment of the less popular girls. Two or three staff members were in the unit at any given time, and Mr. Italy and Scarecrow often worked together.

Sometimes if the Scarecrow would cut me a cigarette for some infraction of attitude, Mr. Italy would find some reason to ferret me off for a 'talk', and reinstate my smoking privilege. I doubt the Scarecrow ever noticed, and I never said anything to anyone about it.

I loved the 'talks' with Mr. Italy, which often ended up with us playing one-on-one volleyball after I vented my woes on him.

He seemed genuine in his concerns for me and empathetic to my feelings. There were other staff members, too, who were kind and well-liked by all of us. Radio Man and Little Man, who often worked together and seemed most tolerant of our musical preferences. They would let us play our

70

tapes most of the day, if we weren't doing school work. The music always helped with the atmosphere of the unit.

You always knew when Radio Man was there in the morning because, instead of the Scarecrow's technique of smashing a pot up and down the hallway of our bedrooms, Radio Man always played his favourite singer, Lionel Richie, over the speakers ten minutes before he'd come up to unlock the doors of our rooms. We always knew it would be a music filled day.

One evening when Mr. Italy, Little Man, and Radio Man were on shift together we made music videos. We had so much fun dressing up in the costumes of our favourite singers, and lip-syncing to their music. We all chose our own songs, and got a chance at directing the group in what we wanted them to do in our music video. We decided where we wanted the camera to be.

I was dressed up as Alice Cooper. I had a homemade top hat and black makeup all over my eyes, like the inside cover of the *Love it to Death* album hanging on my wall at home. I wore a cape, had a cane, and made my video of *Only Women Bleed*.

I had girls lined up as back-up singers. I danced around trying to act like Alice Cooper.

I insisted that the lights be turned on and off for lighting effects and sang at the top of my lungs right over Alice himself. It was terrible, and I wish I had a copy of it today.

Slave to the Farm

Mr. Italy would also periodically set up photo shoots for us. He'd let us get all gussied up and take portraits for our loved ones.

I still have a couple of these beauties and pull them out to look at them every so often. What strikes me most about these photos of myself is how, despite the smile on my face, I look so sad. My eyes seem so far away. The look of quiet desperation is etched into my expression. It's like a picture of a freshly captured wild animal after the drama of the chase has dimmed and the realization of defeat accepted. I loved those pictures for years, but now, I have a hard time looking at them without feeling sorry for the little girl staring at me from her cage.

My first stay in Le Village was about six or eight weeks long. I didn't go home when I was released because my mother didn't want me there. I'm sure the weeks of peace of mind had made her drunk with relief, and she didn't want it to end.

My dad was out of the house, and she and my brothers had settled into a comfortable routine without all my drama fucking things up. I knew she believed I was much safer in the system than wandering the streets, but I felt totally rejected and abandoned.

I ended up staying longer in Village because they couldn't find a bed for me anywhere in an open unit. Finally, the grey van showed up to transport me to a group home in the city.

Slave to the Farm

It was a Friday. I got to Notre Dames des Grace (NDG) group home in the early afternoon before any of the kids were back from school.

The last kid to show up that day was a guy I knew from hanging out at Fairview Shopping Centre in Pointe Claire, and he was as surprised to see me as I was him.

We sat chatting and then snuck away to the basement to smoke a spliff that he had.

Bad idea. We got burnt. A staff caught us red handed with the joint hanging out of my mouth. We were sent to our rooms without dinner, and left to stew about what other punishments might be in store for us.

The next morning, while most of thee kids left for their weekends or went out, I was called into the office and told that they were thinking of sending me up north to The Shawbridge Farm. I was told that a final decision would be made on Monday when my social worker* could be contacted, but that it meant I would probably have to go back to Le Village to wait for a bed to open in either Bailey or Renaissance cottages. I went back to my room knowing I had to run before Monday, and decided I would take the first chance I got.

About an hour later, I just walked out the front doors and headed straight back to the West Island where I had connections.

Slave to the Farm

Slave to the Farm

Slave to the Farm

AC/DC

I was a seasoned runaway, and had been through numerous placements by the time I was arrested and charged with shoplifting and assault. The only crimes I would ever be charged with.

I was caught stealing food and boots out of Woolco on the corner of Ste-Marie and St. Charles Blvd. in Kirkland. The assault charge was because I managed to get away from the female security guard that tried to detain me outside the store. I punched her and got her to let go of my arm, but not my purse.

I never carried my own identification, of course preferring the fakes that proved I was over age, but on that fateful day my ID was in the purse, and the purse was in her hands. I was busted.

Slave to the Farm

I didn't have to face the music though until weeks later when they arrested me for being AWOL from The Farm.

I was sentenced to one hundred hours of community service. I guess giving me time seemed inappropriate. I had already spent almost a year in twenty-four hour lock-up at Le Village.

I was ordered to have testing done at the psychiatric hospital. They performed a number of psychological tests on me, and although I didn't know it at the time, they were considering placing me in Verdun at the Douglas Hospital in the Sterns program.

I went with my mother, and after all the tests were said and done, I was asked to sit in the waiting room. Doctor Goldie, the head juvenile psychiatrist, talked to my mother while I sat eating my nails. I was beginning to get a clue that they might be discussing my placement there in the loony bin. I was panicking.

I had heard horror stories about the Sterns program, which included people being drugged, strapped to beds, forced abortions, psychological humiliation, and shock treatments. I was terrified they were going to say I was crazy.

Finally, I was called into the office where the doctor and my mother sat. My mother looked flustered and agitated. She pulled the seat meant for me closer to her own and I sat down with my heart in my mouth.

Slave to the Farm

"Now Erika, I just have one question for you" the doctor said, not looking up at me.

"Why do you think your mother gives you permission to lie, steal, and beat people up?"

Mom exploded, "Oh for God sakes, I don't have to listen to this anymore. You, doctor, need help. There is something very, very wrong with you. Erika, come on, we are getting out of here." She half pushed, half dragged me out of his office.

My heart filled with joy. I felt like my mother was on my side for once. For the first time, in a very long time, we played for the same team. I held on tight to her as we left the hospital.

"They aren't sending you to that quack, come hell or high water," she said when we got to the car.

So my brush with Montreal's notorious psychiatric hospitals was averted because my mother thought the head of the juvenile psychiatric department was a quack.

The Allen Memorial Institute, funded in part by the Rockefeller Foundation though McGill University, was the same hospital where brainwashing experiments were conducted by Dr. D. Ewen Cameron, President of the American, Canadian and first president of the World Psychiatric Associations. They were CIA-funded experiments, and have since been the subject of many publications.

Slave to the Farm

In Naomi Klein's book, *The Shock Doctrine,* she describes Dr. Cameron's work at the Allen *as "... a scientifically based system for extracting information from 'resistant sources.' In other words, torture."*

Dr. Cameron's Allen Memorial experiments eventually led to the CIA's Counterintelligence Interrogation manual, July 1963.

It was the first manual on how to employ *"coercive counterintelligence interrogation of resistant sources".* Some of the techniques listed are: *'use of electric shock, prolonged constraint, prolonged exertion, extremes of heat, cold, or moisture, deprivation of food or sleep, disrupting routines, solitary confinement, threats of pain, deprivation of sensory stimuli, hypnosis, and use of drugs or placebo'.*

In 1983, this manual was revised and renamed Resource Exploitation Training Manual. It was revised once more in 1985, and is now available for anyone to download and read.

The eerie relevance to the techniques in this manual to my experience in the juvenile system chilled my blood when I read it for the first time. I recognized many of the techniques described being used on me and the troubled teens around me while incarcerated. We were easily described as resistant sources and deprivation was highly effective for achieving institutional goals.

Slave to the Farm

One example that comes to mind is a story told to me in 2006 about a room program that one of the Shawbridge Grads I was interviewing described to me.

He was in Chapel, the maximum security locked unit for boys on The Shawbridge Farm. He was in solitary confinement and they left him there for days without his glasses, the glasses he needed to see his own hands.

He teared up when he recounted the humiliation of it. His anger and frustration at being blinded was mesmerizing behind the thick glasses on his nose that magnified it. He couldn't even remember why he was in solitary in the first place. Fighting, he thought, but they took the glasses because he said he was depressed. They blinded him for his own safety they told him.

Instead they left him with a lifetime of compartmentalized rage that was obvious even to me all those years later.

I'm scared to think of what technological advances they have today in the field of "Human Resource Exploitation", or how they are being used to control children now. Isolation, torture and stigmatization of clinically depressed people still is as relevant today as it was then.

Make no mistake these techniques, used on millions of people worldwide, have lingering social consequences yet to be fully realized.

Slave to the Farm

In 1984, at fourteen, I went AWOL every chance I got. In fact, I went AWOL from every placement I was ever in except Le Village, but I figured out how I could run from there too. I just never had the nerve to try.

During Sunday visits with my parents, we met in the gym, which had three doors into it. One that led to our unit, another that led to the boy's unit and a third that led out into a reception area at the front of the building.

Because we were body-searched after each visit, we were not allowed to return to our units until that search had taken place so during those visiting hours, we had to use the washroom out in the reception area. It was a private bathroom with a single toilet and sink next to a small window with nothing but a screen and the great outdoors beyond.

At barely one hundred pounds, I could fit through that window, no sweat.   The guard at the front desk was the only person who could see out the glass doors. He could have seen me running off, but sometimes he wasn't there, especially after all the visiting families had arrived and were accounted for. I knew it would work but never tried.

The one weekend I was going to do it, fate dealt me a bum hand and the guard never left the front desk. One scheduled visitor didn't show up, so he sat there the whole two hours waiting for them. I never planned to try again.

Slave to the Farm

I went through a few more placements, like a brief stay at Youth Horizons' Mount St. Bruno, but like water running downhill, I finally found myself placed at 'The Farm' in Prevost.

Bailie Cottage was my first placement on The Farm, and my most challenging.

I had already been well seasoned at Le Village to being locked up, but the atmosphere in Bailie was much different.

What I remember most about Bailie Cottage was that you were never alone. There was no privacy there. If you wanted to shave your legs, someone had to supervise, even if you just wanted to soak in a bath, someone was watching. They counted the cutlery before and after every meal to make sure they were all returned, and you couldn't flake out and just read all day like you could in Village. Every minute was scheduled and structured. I felt suffocated there.

I was inspired to write my own poems. I'd written a few in Le Village before I got to The Farm, but I really started writing in earnest in Bailie.

Unfortunately, nothing is left of that poetry now. I never had the secretarial skills or the belief in their value to keep them safe. But if energy is neither created nor destroyed, then I know the effort to write them was well worth it anyway.

I'll always remember poetry classes in the top floor of that unit. Especially sitting in the padded window seat reading Robert Frost's, *The*

Slave to the Farm

Road Not Taken for the first time. It was a rare moment when I was carried away and out into space.

The Frost verse that inspired me most:

> *I shall be telling this with a sigh*
> *Somewhere ages and ages hence:*
> *Two roads diverged in a wood, and I*
> *I took the one less traveled by,*
> *And that has made all the difference.*

Robert Frost

On one AWOL, I hooked up with a boyfriend down at the beach and snuck into his house every night after his mother went to bed. She was a single mom who worked long hours, and was up and out of the house early every morning so never noticed I was there... we thought.

After two weeks of this, she finally came down early one morning and woke us up. She told me to leave or she would call the police. That was all I needed to hightail it out of there, but Chunk tried to reason with her, pleading I had nowhere to go. She wasn't buying it.

"I know her parents live right here in Beaconsfield, she certainly isn't homeless." She just couldn't believe that if she called the police they would bring me to juvy* before they would bring me home.

I left Chunk and his mother arguing, and headed for the beach where I could hang out till Chunk came to find me later.

While waiting for him, I decided to make another run to Sudbury. My cousin had a boyfriend with his own place, and I figured I could just crash there till my aunt could convince my mother to let me stay with them.

Chunk wouldn't hear of it, but I convinced him it was something I had to do. He said he was coming with me then. We went to another of our friends to try and borrow some money, but instead we got a third traveling partner. The guys were both eighteen and at least they could go without risk of arrest.

I don't know how, but the three of us managed to hitch-hike to Sudbury and hook up with my cousin who found us an apartment. The third wheel didn't stay in Ontario long. Only a couple of days later he headed back to Montreal alone. Chunk and I stayed and collected a welfare cheque.

The first week I was in Sudbury, Mary-Jane never told her parents she was seeing me and bringing me food from their larder, but the stress of hearing how distraught my mother was finally made her admit to her own mother that she knew where I was.

My aunt was shocked to hear I was in Ontario again, but Mary-Jane wouldn't tell her exactly where. She held out for a couple of days, but then called to say that my aunt knew where I was, and was coming over.

Chunk and I split right away, and Frog Eyes never saw me. We had been there long enough to make our own connections, so we moved in with a single mom who had a room she would give us for child-minding and yard work.

I never let Mary-Jane know where we were, but I called my aunt to let her know I was still there and all right. I asked if she would speak to my mother again, but she already had. My mother wanted me back in Montreal.

Eventually, Chunk wanted to go home too. We were broke and struggling with our roommate, so one day we just decided to head back.

His mom, true to her word called the police when she found us sleeping after our long trip back. I was arrested and brought to L'Escale for a night in the stainless room.

I was then deposited back into Le Village to start the longest stint in lock-up I would ever do.

I was a seasoned veteran this time around. I sailed through the three-day isolation period with no flies on me and was reintegrated into the group like I'd never left. I'd been gone only a few short months.

Most of the girls had changed. It seemed less cliquey somehow. The turnover in a place like Le Village was quite high. It was supposed to be

just a transitional placement, somewhere to park a
kid while they waited for a bed somewhere else, but
a small core group stayed in Village for quite a
while when I was there. I met a lot of girls who I
would later live with on The Farm, but I never felt
as close to them as I did in Le Village.

I went through a number of roommates, and
learned some disturbing stories about the way other
families operated.

I met Meow, the first child prostitute I've
ever known, as well as Miss Calvin Klein, the first
person I met who had ever killed someone. There
was Sneakers, who had been abused sexually and
physically most of her young life, and Missy, who I
would AWOL with a year later. Mafia Babe,
another good friend I met in Village, has made
appearances in my life ever since. Lizard would be
waiting for me in Renaissance when I finally got
there.

These were my friends, but there were
dozens of other girls that I shared intimate and
memorable moments with in those hazy, confusing,
dark days of my youth.

Lollipop was my first roommate in Lachine
Shelter. I met her again almost a year later in Le
Village. There was a buzz in the unit because a new
girl was processed and in the orientation room.
Later as we filed by, she was staring out her tiny
window at us.

From the outside of that little window, all
you see are the eyes of an individual who has just

been through a practiced destabilization procedure. The eyes that gaze out don't always look human, and hers certainly did not.

Her eyes looked like the eyes of a hyena, all wild, and bloodshot, and yellow. I certainly didn't recognize her that morning staring out from that tiny window. I didn't recognize her that night either. I got to my door, only to find a girl lying on the bed in my room, vacant until then.

She was pretending to sleep or meditate or something so she didn't look up at me right away.

I still didn't recognize her as I stared at her. She had changed so much in the last year: her hair, her face, her body. It wasn't until she looked up and recognized me that I knew who she was. She had changed her name, and the staff had called her Trixie when they told us about her at breakfast. She would always be Lollipop to me, but I promised not to say anything.

She was a completely different girl than the one I had met before. We talked long into the night about the months she'd spent in New York City, and how it had changed her. She was a prostitute now, and had learned how to do muggings. She mainlined cocaine, and confided in me that her pimp was working on getting her out as soon as possible. He was going to pretend he was her father or uncle or brother.

I sat dumbstruck by her stories, horrified at the brutality of them. How they had beaten a guy to near death, and done armed robberies. She had ripped the diamond earrings out of a woman's ears right on the street in Manhattan.

I was a little afraid of her, and didn't want to believe what she was saying to me, but she never noticed and just kept on talking.

Lollipop's orientation was short because a new girl was hot on her heels, very pregnant and in need of the orientation room to dry out from heroin.

Red was my first pregnant heroin addict, and thankfully she didn't last a week. None of us were sad to see her, her addiction, or her bad attitude, go. We all felt really sorry for that baby, though.

Lollipop and I didn't remain roommates for very long. I'm not sure how, but her pimp did manage to get her back into his clutches and right back on the streets.

I would meet her again one day on the corner of Ste. Catherine and St. Laurent, but that is a story for later.

One of the many stories Meow told me about prostituting for her mother went like this. Her mother used to bring men home to the apartment. She would service the men interested in young girls, or her mother would do the job. Sometimes they would worked together for extra bling.*

One day a 'regular' came to the door while Mom was out, and Meow liking the guy let him in.

"It was like a regular blow job, you know, and he was real quick about it, so that's why I liked him...anyway, usually he just left the room when it was finished, but 'cause mom wasn't there he handed me the money! It was $30 bucks... just for doing that! It was so easy. I never told mom about it when she came back. I started doing for myself after school when she wasn't home, just to make money, you know. You should try it; you could make a lot of money too!"

I don't know how long she had been in the sex trade before she realized that someone was being paid for what she was doing, but what baffled me even more was that she didn't seem angry about being used that way.

In fact, she seemed happy to have finally learned the big secret of how to survive in this world. It was the moment she became a 'real' self-supporting woman. She was a professional before the tender age of fifteen. Ain't life grand?

At that point in my life, the idea of exchanging sex for money was new. I had never even considered it, didn't know that people did such a thing, and because it was just a few months after my rape, I found the idea of being paid for sex repulsive. Paying for it seemed very wrong. and liking to be paid for it seemed even more troubling. I was resourceful, however, so I tucked that little wad of information away for further consideration. Who knew if it would come in handy someday? That was the beauty of entering the lion's den as a kitten. All the big cats are more than willing to share the litter box with you, as long as you save them a piece of your steak... or a cigarette, and I had lots of cigarettes. I was the poor little rich kitten.

Mafia Babe was paraded past us into the office one evening while we were all having dinner. We were all a little confused because she didn't look at all like a teen. In fact, at first we thought she was a parent or maybe a social worker.

She was wearing a mink coat, a couple of pounds of make-up and had her hair streaked grey. Everything about her reeked of big bucks.

After the intake procedures she was left alone in the orientation room for her three-day orientation program. What I remember most of that time was how she never was there in the window sharing out at us. She was like a ghost behind that door.

I was never chosen to bring meals to her so the first time I saw her knocked off her pedestal was after her room program was over.

She was being introduced to us at smoke time one morning. She chose her poison and sat down as far from any of us as possible. She didn't make eye contact with anyone, and acted as if we were about as interesting as dog shit on her Gucci shoes.

I decided I would talk to her, and try to make her comfortable. After saying hello, I was rewarded with the coldest stare and told, "I won't be needing any friends in this shit hole!"

Slave to the Farm

It stung, and after my own fuck you, I retreated, hoping she'd choke on something at lunch.

She had stamina and remained aloof and distant for days before she broke. She spoke to no one, she didn't participate in any card games or sports activities. The staff quit sending her to her room when they realized that was exactly what she wanted. Cutting her cigarettes didn't seem to faze her, either. She was a stone, but like any mountain, eventually time grinds you down to dust.

Maybe because I was the first to make an attempt at friendship, she approached me. I was playing solitaire, and she came over and challenged me to a card game. I kind of nonchalantly dealt us a hand of Rummy, and we played, not really talking much.

All the girls whispered and snickered to each other when they saw us sitting there together. Somewhere in the third or fourth hand, she said, "Hey, I'm sorry about that first day. I know you were just trying to be nice."

"Whatever" was all I could come up with. I wasn't about to be stung by her viper tongue again, and sat on guard there with her.

We fell into a quiet comfortable camaraderie in the following weeks. We sat next to each other at meals, always played on the same teams, and spent hours killing time with cards or backgammon.

She never really told me what her story was, and I could tell she wasn't the least bit interested in mine. I did know she was obsessed by anything Mafia-like, or remotely Italian.

We shared books like Mario Puzo's *"The Sicilian"*, and *"The Last Don"*, and she would dreamily talk of how she wished she could have been born Italian, and how unfair it was that she had an English name.

One day she asked me if I had heard the name Cotroni before. It sounded familiar, but I wasn't sure where I'd heard it.

"Cotroni, the mob boss?" she added helpfully.

I said maybe I'd read something in the paper, or saw him on the news, but no, I didn't know it.

"Well, I work for them. His son bought my coat."

I was impressed. I believed her because I could still see her all dolled up on that first day, looking like a Mafia wife.

She continued, "I work as a bartender in a couple of their bars in St. Leonard."

She told me as soon as she got out she was going right back to them and asking for help. She never spoke about her parents or about going back to live with them. Going back to the mob was all she talked about. I asked her if she did tricks for them, and she was horrified.

"I'm no fucking whore! Actually, when I get out, I'm going to open a whore house and get all these dumb bitches to work for me. I'll treat them better than any of those scummy pimps downtown."

Slave to the Farm

She said she would cut me in. We could get rich being "Escort Providers". We would drive fancy cars, have tons of expensive clothes, and eat out every day in high class restaurants.

We made up business plans to pitch to the Cotronis. She was positive they would lend us the money to get started.

She was convinced that she was going to marry a Mafia Boss. It all sounded like a fairy tale to me, but I went along with everything she said. The weeks flew by as we plotted and planned, and the day of her transfer to The Farm loomed larger.

I was heartbroken when she was shipped out to Bailie Cottage on The Farm. I would never see her behind locked doors again.

The next time I laid eyes on her was in one of the mafia owned bars in the Italian district of St. Leonard, years later.

In Le Village, we often got to be roommates with the girls we hung out with. I'm guessing it was to avoid friction in the rooms at night. So Lizard and I shared a room for the last couple of weeks of her stay before she transferred to The Farm.

About a week before her transfer we hatched a plan for me to smuggle cigarettes from my weekly visit, so we could have a smoke after lights out in our room: sort of a send-off celebration. I managed to smuggle two cigarettes back into the unit.

We were locked in our rooms for an hour every day from 3pm to 4pm while the staff did shift change. We used this time to hide them in our base board radiator and started working on the problem of getting a lighter we could use.

That turned out to be much more challenging than we first anticipated. It was a couple of days before we managed to procure one, and three days before she was scheduled to transferred to The Farm.

The cigarettes had been lying in wait, and our anticipation had grown to monumental proportions.

It was the Scarecrow's chain smoking that provided the lighter. He used to leave his cigarettes on the table sometimes. Lizard walked by and palmed the lighter when she thought no one was looking. She was wrong.

Cat Eyes saw her do it, and unbeknownst to us, went straight to Scarecrow. He put two and two together, and went immediately to search our room. He found the cigarettes, and called us out of the classroom to confront us.

We sat like hardened criminals before him, and refused to talk. Just a couple of blank walls. Our punishment was a five day room program. Five days of total segregation. Lizard really only had two full days left, but spent those alone in the orientation room while I was left to rot in our bedroom.

On the morning of her transfer, the grey bus came to pick her up and I sat crying while I listened to her door being opened. I strained to see out the window for a glimpse of her, but could only see the door of the room next to mine. She called out to me as she was hurried away down the stairs, and I gloated for hours at her last act of defiance, but I didn't dare answer.

Those were the hardest five days I did in the system. Five full days with no human contact except to deliver food. There were no books, no pens or paper, no Sunday visit and no cigarettes. It ate at my soul. I cried for hours and slept as much as I could, but nothing took away the edgy hysteria simmering under the surface. I felt panic raise up from my bowels for no apparent reason, and became weepy and frightened at all sorts of familiar sounds. At night, I dreamed of being choked, or drowned, or paralyzed. I could not calm my thoughts, and felt near psychotic at times. I thought of Squaw, and even scratched myself to see if it would help. Oddly, it did feel better to bleed on to the sheets: physical evidence of my pain.

Finally, the last night crested, and I knew I would be able to join the other girls in the morning. My nerves calmed, and I vowed to pull myself together. I would not let anyone know how hard it had been for me. My stress ulcer was born, but I made it through the night, and once again emerged from that locked room a changed person.

When I got into circulation again, the buzz was that the guys in Dara, another locked unit on

Slave to the Farm

The Farm, had just gotten the right to have eight cigarettes a day!

We would continue to get only six. Almost as retaliation for the room program, and the loss of the two cigarettes, I started a campaign to get the same amount of smokes as the boys.

All the girls wrote letters, which we then submitted to the Le Village staff to bring to their monthly meetings with Head Honcho the Director of Youth Protection. We demanded a group meeting with him ourselves.

We had group meetings all the time, but they weren't something we enjoyed. Your faults were aired out for everyone to pick apart, and they were time consuming and emotional. Often they left you feeling drained and deflated. But this one was different. It was our agenda we would be discussing.

We all took our turns stating the reason we believed we should be entitled to the same amount of smokes as the guys.

I asked what the justification was for the unequal treatment, and was told that the boys were more likely to have violent outbursts, and needed to be distracted more.

"Bullshit!" we cried. "Sexual discrimination!" we whined. We got our extra two cigarettes, but only for those of us on the higher privilege levels.

I'd loss all my privileges because of the room program, but chalked it up to a victory all the same. It would only be a matter of time till I gained my privilege levels again.

The cigarette coup didn't sit well with the staff though. Soon I had Cat Eyes as a roommate.

She was the in-house-tattle-tail, one of Scarecrow's favourites, and not to be trusted with anything. So I guess she was there to keep an eye on me, and give regular reports on my schemes. I just learned to lay low, and tell her nothing.

After the turbulent waters calmed, and the winds of dissent quieted, the roommate shuffle realigned itself, and Sneakers became my new roommate.

Sneakers was a special case. She was extremely quiet and rarely smiled or even talked. She was deadly serious all the time, and very much a loner. She was secretive and paranoid with a beaten-dog quality about her. She would sneak every bite of food into her mouth at the dinner table because she didn't like to eat in front of anyone. She'd cover her mouth with one hand while stuffing tiny morsels of food in with the other when she thought no one was looking. She also never let anyone see her naked.

Three girls at a time showered in a large tiled shower room. There were three cubicles with no doors. Sneakers would hide in one of them, hanging her towel to block our view, till we were gone, then undress and shower alone.

Slave to the Farm

The staff indulged her in this. None of the other girls got that privilege, but we didn't really care. We just wondered what the big deal was.

One night, I asked her what her problem was, and although she was reluctant to talk about it I just kept hounding away at her. I promised I wouldn't tell anyone. I told her it couldn't be that big of a deal. I finally broke her, and she stripped down to let me look at her body.

I was struck speechless. To date, I have never seen so many scars on one body. Burns, bites, scratches and stitches like train tracks covering her body. I stood staring at her with my mouth hanging open.

"It's not that bad." I croaked out unconvincingly, and she smiled at me, I'm sure to make me feel better. She had obvious human bite marks on each of her butt cheeks, and more than twenty cigarette burns on her arms, legs, and back. But the one in the centre of her back is a snap shot in my memory I cannot erase. It was certainly done by someone else, and it looked like the fattest cigar ever rolled was stubbed out in her tender young flesh. I dry-heaved at the sight of it.

Her arms where covered with slash marks, some self-inflicted, some not. She told me proudly that the half inch scar on her forearm was when she cut herself to the bone. I wanted to cry and hold her and kill whoever had done that to her. She just smiled her sad smile at me and got dressed.

Slave to the Farm

We lay down to sleep, but I couldn't. I just didn't understand how that could be done to a young girl. I couldn't understand why she was the one locked up in jail. I started to cry softly, and she crawled into my bed, and put her arms around me. She lovingly rubbed my hair and back, and said soothing things to me.

Suddenly, I noticed a change in her. Her breathing changed, and she tried to kiss me. I went along with it at first, but almost immediately started pulling away from her.

"What the fuck are you doing?" I barked at her, and she cowered away to her own bed.

"I just thought I could make you feel better."

"Well, don't. OK?"

She rolled over and went to sleep. I lay awake for hours wondering what had just happened. Was I a lesbian? There was a second there when I wanted to kiss her. I wanted her to rub me and make me feel better. What's the matter with me?

The next morning when that key hit the door, I awoke again to a new me.

Needle And The Damage Done

NEIL YOUNG

My health wasn't the greatest when I was a teenager, and while I lived in the system I was plagued by severe migraines.

Now, after two drug-free births, I would never categorize labour pain as the 'worst you can experience', but those migraines would definitely rate on that scale.

I had one about every two weeks, sometimes more, sometimes less. I was given Tylenol for the pain, but it never helped.

I would just wither in my bed begging to die. Anything to make that pain stop. No medical cause could be found for them. I was told they were stress-related, psychosomatic, and all in my head. I'll say they were all in my head!

Anyone who has these kinds of migraines can probably relate. For those who haven't experienced them, they are as difficult to watch as they are painful. I would hold my head as tightly as I could, and ball up in a fetal position rocking back and forth, moaning and groaning for hours. Some people were sympathetic, others not so.

Slave to the Farm

Some believed I was just trying to get attention. The Le Village nurses were concerned enough, however, to order more tests, so an electroencephalogram (EEG) was scheduled, and the grey van arrived at Le Village to pick me up.

I was taken to the Douglas Hospital again for tests, but only normal brain activity was noted. The hospital staff suggested I have another EEG, while I was asleep at a later date. This posed a bit of a challenge to the Le Village staff.

There were two shifts in a day, 7 a.m. to 3 p.m. and 4 p.m. To 10 p.m., but overnight, there was simply a night watchman on duty. The only time I ever saw this guard was when I had to go to the washroom after the staff left. If I didn't catch him on his round along the hall where our bedrooms were, I had to stomp on the floor so he could hear and come upstairs from the common room downstairs.

For the second EEG, I was supposed to stay awake for a full twenty-four hours or more, then go to the hospital early in the morning, have the electrodes attached to my head, and try to sleep. Not an easy task for me at the best of times.

I got the privilege of sitting in the common room all night watching TV with the guard. It was a long boring night, but we made it through without either of us falling sleep and in the wee hours of the dark morning, the grey van came to transport me to the hospital.

Slave to the Farm

The process of attaching all those electrodes to my head took some time, but eventually I was left in the dark to sleep.

It wasn't easy. I was tired, but I just lay there filled with anxiety, struggling to relax with all these wires stuck to me. Three or four times nurses came into the room to check if I was asleep yet, and were surprised to see me awake each time.

I did fall asleep finally, but twice I woke to flashing strobe lights in my face. I didn't see anyone in the room with me, but it seemed as if someone knew I was awake. The strobing would stop. I would relax again, fall asleep, and then be woken up again with disco lights flashing at me. I didn't understand what was going on, but tried to ignore the lights and fall asleep again.

I was finally deeply asleep and resting comfortably when a sharp pain hit me like a sledge hammer in the centre of my skull. I woke up with my eyes rolling back in my head, and grabbed for my face.

I met another hand in the dark as I grabbed onto a tube being shoved into my nose. My heart leaped into my mouth as I realized I wasn't alone in the room. The tube was wrenched from my hand as I rolled over to get a look at the person with me. It was dark, so all I could make out was a shadowy shape that I knew was a man.

"What are you doing?" I screeched at him, but he just spun on his heels heading for the door. As he pulled it open the light from outside spilt into

105

the dark room. I got a brief look at him. He was in his mid-30's, had thick pop bottle glasses, and was wearing a white lab coat. He never looked at me or said a word, but I knew he hadn't expected me to wake up. He was trying to get out of the room before I became more agitated or asked any more questions.

I started to scream. I was terrified. What the hell had just happened? I was awake and fully confused now. I had these electrodes stuck to my head, and they were attached to a machine recording my brain patterns. I felt like I was on a leash. I couldn't go after him and I'm not sure I would have anyway. All the yelling soon brought a nurse into the room to see what had happened. She tried to calm me, but I was hysterical. I tried to tell her what I had just experienced. She was skeptical and told me over and over to just relax.

"Some man was just in here trying to put a tube in my nose." I tried to convince her, but she told me it was all a dream. No one could possibility have been in the room with me.

I got more hysterical, and started pulling the electrodes off my head. There was no way I was staying in that room for a second longer. She tried to stop me while calling for help. Mayhem ensued as the room began to full with medical staff.

I wanted out of there, I wanted no more to do with any of them. No one believed me. I know what I saw and felt. My nose was sore, my heart raced, and the EEG was over. They agreed to take all the electrodes off my head and let me sit in a waiting room in the hall till the grey van returned to pick me up. I finally calmed down.

I sat and suspected every white-coat who passed me in the hall, but never laid eyes on him again.

I was relieved to make it back to Le Village, and never mentioned what happened at the hospital to any of the staff.

One of the unit nurses who had suggested the EEG in the first place, was the only one to mention the test to me a week later. She told me she heard I had a nightmare and asked me what happened. I just shrugged and said, "I don't know." She didn't probe.

The migraines continued through my whole institutional life, but after the tests I got a 'migraine prescription'. It made me dopey and only helped if I took it early enough.

Another chronic problem I had while in the system was irregular periods. Sometimes I could go six months without bleeding, then get my period and bleed for six weeks. There was no telling when I would get it, or for how long.

The menstrual cycles of all the girls seem to sync up into the cliques that formed socially. The more you hung out with someone, the more likely you were to bleed with them.

I was an outcast. My hormones didn't seem to want to identify with anyone.

Slave to the Farm

At one point all the girls in the unit were put on the pill whether they were sexually active or not. I found it humiliating and those little devils always made me sick to my stomach. We would all line up to get our pills in the evening. I hated it. I was sure they gave me migraines too. They did help regulate my periods sometimes, but I would often just palm the tiny pill and flush it down the toilet. I still would bleed excessively or not bleed at all so the staff paid more attention to whether I was taking my pills or not. I would have to put it on my tongue and then stick it out for them to see. Being caught not taking them meant being cut cigarettes, so I just took the pills. It was easier, but I always felt like I was about to barf.

Every once in a while a group of girls would all be loaded into one of those grey vans and taken into the heart of Montreal to see the gynecologist. There was a clinic right up the street from The Montreal Children's Hospital, on Atwater. All the girls saw this tiny little woman named Dr. Q. We had paps done, and got prescriptions for birth control. Had our breasts and armpits kneaded, and were told we were infertile. Well I was anyway.

Dr. Q told me that I might have children with the aid of medication, but it wasn't a guarantee. There was nothing she could do. It was very important to continue taking birth control pills to regulate my period, she said, but forget having babies.

I didn't know whether to be devastated or relieved. I quit taking the pill as soon as I could. She was wrong of course. I had my first healthy baby at twenty-eight, and my second at thirty-two. I've never understood her logic behind cursing a teenage girl with such a false sense of security in her own infertility though. So convinced I was I couldn't get pregnant that when I did, it took three positive results from three different sources for me to believe it. It was just dumb luck I didn't get pregnant earlier.

Slave to the Farm

TAKE THE LONG WAY HOME

Supertramp

By the time I was released from Le Village after my seven month stint, I was well conditioned in institutional life. The sound of a key hitting a locked door was seared into my subconscious, as well as the habit of never entering a room without being invited in.

There are so many do's and don'ts in the system; it becomes confusing when you are expected to make your own decisions about your daily life again. At home with my mother and brothers, I was kind of lost and edgy. I didn't feel comfortable anymore with my homey surroundings, and asked my mother for every piece of food I ate, coffee I drank, or shower I took.

Slave to the Farm

She didn't really understand this inability to assimilate into the routine of our family life. My difficulties making the transition weighed on everyone. It wasn't long before I was in trouble with drinking, drugs and missing again.

Around this time I showed up at Diz's high school in Dorval, and told her I was taking off again. She asked where I was planning on going, but I didn't have any answers for her.

"Anywhere away from here", was all I could come up with. She suggested that we go to Wells Beach, Maine to see her summertime boyfriend.

It was the first time she ever talked about running away to anywhere so I was surprised at her suggestion, but I of course loved the idea and excitedly agreed.

She packed up her school bag, and we headed to her mother's to get some supplies. We stuffed a back-pack full of clothes and booze, forgetting to add enough food or water for the journey, and loaded the 40 lb. bag onto my slight frame.

We headed over to a little send-off party at our friends and said good-bye to everyone. We listened to music and had a couple of drinks while they all made fun of our plans to head towards the U.S. border.

"How do you guys think you are going to get in? Just walk right through the border crossing, or are you hoping to hop over a fence somewhere in the woods?"

Slave to the Farm

Ha, ha they all got a good laugh at us, but we left Beaconsfield heading to the Champlain Bridge on our way off the island, and to the excited States.*

Our first hurdle was the bridge itself. We didn't have a car, so we tried walking across it. This bridge sees 160,000 crossings on any given day, and none of those are walking. We were still on the approach leading onto the bridge when we got our first ride. A white cargo van pulled over in front of us, and hurriedly waved us into his truck.

"Are you guys fucking crazy? You can't walk across Champlain Bridge. You'll get killed!" He barked at us in a french accent as he pulled out into the rolling traffic again. We just shrugged it off and thanked him. He continued to throw head-shaking glances at us.

"Where you girls off to?"

We told him of our plans to go to Wells Beach, and asked him if he knew where we could easily slip over the border.

He laughed at us as if remembering a time when he himself used to do crazy things like that, and told us he knew a perfect place. He said he refused to take us across the line himself but would get us to somewhere we could.

I don't remember the name of the town, but he let us out in this small hamlet where all the cars on the south side of the street had New York plates, and those on the north side sported Quebec plates.

Slave to the Farm

Diz and I wandered up and down the street trying to figure out how to get across as he drove off.

A small car pulled up alongside us after not too long. The driver was a young guy, and asked if we needed help. We told him we wanted to get across the border, and did he know a place we could sneak over. He told us to get in, and he would bring us to a trail that the locals use.

We piled into his tiny Honda Civic, and he brought us to a trail-head somewhere out of town. He pointed to the dirt track and told us it was a five minute walk through the woods. He agreed to pick us up on the other side.

We headed off into the woods, chatting away until I noticed we were no longer on the path. We started to worry. We scoured the ground looking for the path that had been plainly marked when we entered the woods, but now somehow eluded us.

Diz starting to really panic, and was quickly becoming hysterical. She started to scream "help!" at the top of her lungs. Not knowing what to do, or wanting to get caught by border security, I walked up to her and slapped her hard across the face as I'd seen done in many movies to calm someone down. It did the trick. She stopped screaming. I felt bad, but I needed her to stop screaming so I could think of what to do next.

"Just listen for cars. The road has to be somewhere close," I said.

Slave to the Farm

Listening hard, we heard a transport truck roll by somewhere to the right of us, and I headed towards the sound with Diz following close behind.

Not far from that spot, we came upon a four foot tall split rail fence. We climbed over it and found the dirt path again. We weren't sure if it was the right path, or which way we should follow it, but didn't care as long as we found our way out of the woods.

It was dusk when we came out onto a country road. We didn't see anyone or any houses. We didn't even have a clue which country we were in. We were sure the guy who had offered to pick us up had left, and gone home. We stood at the tree line wondering what to do.

I spied a car at the crest of the next hill, a good kilometre up the road. Neither of us could be sure of the make of the car, so didn't know whether to flag it down.

I told her to stay hidden, and I would get closer to see if it was our knight in vehicle amour, but the reverse lights on the car came on first, and it began backing up.

Diz was sure it was him, but I had visions of the cops coming to arrest us and considered running back into the woods.

Just as I was about to run, I could see that she was right. It was the little Civic. We waited at the tree line till he backed right up to us.

"What on earth took you guys so long?" he said as we piled in. We told him how we got lost, and he shook his head. He said he couldn't see for the life of him how that had happened; the path was straight. Either way, we'd made it. We were in the United States.

We made a deal with the guy: we would fill his tank with the very little money we had, and he would drive us till his gas tank was half full, then drop us off with enough gas to get back.

It was well into the evening when he dropped us off at the St. Johnsbury, Vermont 7-11 convenience store, where many young people were hanging out.

We walked up to them, and struck up a conversation. We told them we needed a safe place to spend the night where the cops wouldn't find us. Very few of the kids had ever even met a Canadian. Diz and I were shocked. It made us instant celebrities.

They all started thinking of places we could stay. Finally, they agreed to walk us to a baseball field that had dugouts that were covered and private. They left us there, and I laid down on one of the benches feeling exhaustion wash over me.

Diz, on the other hand, paced like a caged lion.

"What was that?" she whispered at every night sound.

"Diz, just lay down and relax. We are all good here. Get some sleep, and at first light we'll hit the road again."

Slave to the Farm

I tried to reassure her, and she did finally lay down after retrieving her Swiss Army knife from our bag and laying it across her chest. We grew quiet, and were almost asleep when we both heard footsteps on the path above our dugout.

We stayed as quiet as possible, not wanting to be discovered, but within moments a guy stuck his head in, spied us, and yelled "Over here!"

It was a guy from the 7-11, with four other people.

"We thought we would just come and get you guys, and bring you over to our apartment for the night. You guys are probably hungry, and it can get pretty cold out here."

We gratefully collected up our belongings and followed the crowd back to a building, heavy with the stench of recent fumigation.

"Don't worry about the smell, they just sprayed for roaches," the little lady of the house said over her shoulder to us.

The apartment was small and barren. Two bedrooms, one empty, and a larger kitchen/living room with nothing but a table and chairs in it. The bathroom was only a closet with leaky faucets and a toilet that constantly ran.

They made us sandwiches and offered us watery American beer, which I refused, but Diz accepted happily.

We sat around smoking cigarettes and leafy pot, talking until both Diz and I could hardly keep our eyes open. Finally, Diz and I lay down in an empty bedroom to sleep, while the others balled up in other corners. I woke abruptly to Diz kicking and struggling with a dark figure that had crawled into the room.

I screamed, "What's going on?" and the dark figure quickly retreated. Diz just clung to me and me to her, and together we watched him go.

"Who was that?" I asked her, but she just shook her head looking like she was about to cry.

"I don't know, but it creeped me out," she said.

"It's OK, we're fine now."

We just lay there afterwards, spooning each other for protection and warmth. The rising sun began peeking in the window, but finally I managed to fall back into a fitful half sleep until Diz heard someone out in the kitchen and woke me up.

We had toast and coffee for breakfast. The couple who lived in the apartment offered to drive us out to the highway. The four of us piled into an old muscle car, a Charger I think, and headed off down the road to the nearest gas station.

After filling the tank, the driver turned to us and said he was going to do us a favor and drive us right to the Vermont/Maine border. It was great news. We were surprised and thankful. We settled back in for the ride, but somewhere in the middle of White Mountain National Forest, the car started to blow smoke from under the hood. We pulled over and Mr. 7-11 took a look under the hood.

Slave to the Farm

"End of the road, ladies, this boat is turning around," he informed us while popping the trunk to get our back pack.

We weren't all that disappointed. We were much closer to Maine, so we thanked them profusely and waved goodbye as they sped away back to St. Johnsbury.

We would soon realize that we weren't as well off as we thought. We hoisted the heavy back pack onto my back and started walking. And we walked, and we walked some more. Hours unfolded beneath our feet, and we never saw a single car come by. I was so thirsty my tongue began swelling in my mouth. We had brought no water with us.

The heavy bag in the scorching mid-day sun got passed back and forth between us every five or ten minutes, until we could no longer carry it. We had to sit down; we were so thirsty and grumpy.

By this time, we were cursing the couple for leaving us in the middle of a deserted forest with no water. We considered going into the woods in search of a stream or anything we could quench our thirst with, but before we could get up the nerve to enter into the canopy, we heard a vehicle coming our way. We couldn't tell what direction it was traveling; it was just a distant roar among the trees, and our hearts sunk when it crested the hill traveling in the opposite direction. We watched it race by us with questioning stares from its driver, but his curiosity didn't apply pressure to his brake pedal.

119

Slave to the Farm

He just went on wondering, and we sat there withering into road side raisins.

The car did raise our hopes that another would come by soon, and we never entertained the idea that it wouldn't stop for us when it did. We never did find any water, but a short time later we again heard the rumble of a car engine echoing off the forest. We waited with our hearts in our mouths, hoping this was our ticket out of there.

Like a beacon of light from the heaven's themselves, a big old Monte Carlo came barreling over the crest of the hill heading towards Maine. We both stood up waving our arms so the driver had a good long time to see us there, stranded on the side of the road. We were rewarded with the sound of the engine slowing down. The car pulled over to the shoulder just past us, and we ran over to the passenger side window to ask him for a ride.

"What y'all doing in the middle of nowhere?" he said with a thick Texan accent while reaching over to open the door inviting us in. We climbed in, spewing our story of being left with no water, and how we were on our way to Wells Beach. He gave us water, and told us we were in luck. He was going to Fryburg, Maine, a small town just over the border.

Diz was in the front with Cowboy, and I lounged in the huge back seat, relaxed and content. After a stint of silence with nothing but John Cougar Mellencamp crooning out of the radio,

Cowboy leaned over, reached under his seat and pulled out a big bag of bud.

"You girls get high?" he asked tossing the bag at Diz. She nodded yes, and started to roll a joint. He took and inspected the result.

"Girl, this ain't no joint. It's a tooth pick. It must be one of them ol' Canadian joints, 'cause it ain't no Texan joint. Gimme that bag, darling."

He rolled a joint worthy of being called 'Sir', while driving with his knee, and lit it while turning up the radio. We smoked the high test pot with him and I found myself floating away into la la land.

Diz pocketed the Canadian tooth pick, and headed out on her own journey. I was so relaxed I fell asleep in the back seat, and didn't perk up till he was pulling into the township of Fryburg. He drove us down Main Street to the Pine Grove Cemetery, and let us out at a park next door.

Diz called BeachBoy in Wells Beach, and was told to stay right where we were. After work, he and his friend would drive up to get us.

We settled into the park to wait, and started drinking the gin we had lifted from Diz's stepfather. We hadn't eaten anything all day except the toast early that morning, and after trying to smash cans open with rocks, and only managing to dent them badly, we finally figured out how to use Diz's jack knife can opener.

We sat eating cold ravioli from the can, and it felt good to put something in our tummy. We were getting really tipsy off the straight gin, and the food helped a bit, but by the time BeachBoy and his friend got to the park, Diz and I were stinking drunk.

I hardly remember the trip to Wells Beach, or anything we did when we got there. What I do remember about the first night was waking up early the next morning.   I came to myself with my face wedged into the back of a sofa, and a heavy-weight boxer beating on my brain. I heard someone making coffee in the kitchen and rolled over to see who it was. Standing there in the living room looking down on me was a female Maine State Patrol Officer.

"Hi, you must be Erika," she said, extending her hand to shake mine. I didn't say anything, but reached out to offer her my shaky hand.

"I'm BeachBoy's mom. Sorry I woke you up. You look like you need the sleep. I'm just heading out to work so make yourself at home. See ya later."

I was speechless. I heard a Harley start up outside and pull away. Whoever was in the kitchen making coffee had disappeared out the door before her and left in a truck.

"Diz?" I screamed out, searching through the trailer for her. I found her in the bedroom at the very end of the hall. Groggy and half asleep, she asked what I wanted.

"You didn't tell me we were running away to a cop's house..." I fumed at her.

"No big deal, she's cool."

"Well, you could have told me, I nearly shit my pants when she said my name!"

We spent two weeks in Wells Beach, not getting arrested because of some strike concerning the exchange of information between the Quebec and American authorities.

We hung out with the guys and drove around sightseeing, and one day we went out target shooting. I learned that day how dangerous firearms can be, even in the hands of someone you trust.

The noise, the smell, it all seemed so wrong. I couldn't believe that we weren't doing something illegal. I kept expecting the cops to show up any second. After beer drinking and watching the guys blow away every empty can in sight, BeachBoy asked if I wanted to try it out. I didn't want to shoot the huge double-barrel shotgun, especially not after watching the kickback it had, said "no thanks".

Diz, on the other hand, was loving it. She most certainly wanted to try. There were four or five of us leaning up against the car. Diz and BeachBoy were ten or fifteen feet away. Their backs to us.

He was explaining what to do, showing her all the bells and whistles, then he handed her the gun and showed her how to hold it. He came to stand back with us near the front bumper of the car.

Diz stood there holding the gun, getting comfortable. We couldn't see her face or what was going on in her eyes, but suddenly she raised the

123

gun to her shoulder as if to shoot. She spun the barrel around towards us.

Like a thunderclap the guys hit the dirt, and crawled away to get out of the line of fire. I just stood there, not recognizing the danger. Finally I dropped to the ground and tried to get under the car. There was a look on her face that I had never seen before, a distant, dreamy gaze. She took a couple of steps towards the car searching for something unseen on the ground, pointing the gun purposefully at it.

There was an electric panicky energy in the air, and time slowed down. I had trouble making sense of what people were shouting. She also seemed confused and not sure what to do. She still held the gun with her finger on the trigger pointing in our direction.

BeachBoy had jumped across the hood of the car, and was crouched behind it. He was screaming at her to put the gun on the hood of the car.

"Just put it down." he said extending his arm across the hood towards her. She looked right at him and seemed to come back to herself. He said it again slowly, more calmly, "Just put it down." She walked over and laid the gun on the hood of the car without having taken a shot. He grabbed on to it and immediately cracked it open, unloading the slug. He disappeared with it while I crawled out from under the car, and ran over to Diz.

Slave to the Farm

"Are you OK? What just happened there? You looked like you were going to shoot someone." I peppered her with my questions while she tried to composed herself. She just kept saying "I don't know, I don't know, I don't know."

An argument grew louder near the trunk of the car. One of BeachBoy's friends was really upset, and screaming at him.

"What the fuck, man? She's fucking crazy, man." BeachBoy just spun on his heels heading for the driver's seat. "Get in." He ordered us.

We both climbed into the back seat and one of the crew got in the front with BeachBoy. BeachBoy started the car, blasted the music up high, and peeled out on the dirt road spraying gravel behind us. We didn't say anything to each other, just listened to the loud music, and recovered from the endorphin overdose. By the time we made it to BeachBoy's trailer we had all calmed down, and no one spoke about what had gone on earlier.

A couple of days later, I saw my parent's car coming up the drive. They had driven the long hours to come and get us. We packed up, said our good-byes, and headed north.

In all the snapshots of memories, I always try to remember what happened when my parents finally got me: what they said to me or the people around me. But it's like white noise. It's like not being present at the event. I don't remember. What I do remember is dropping Diz off at her mother's house with a big banner hanging across the front

Slave to the Farm

that said 'Welcome Home Diz We Missed You',
then continuing on with my parents to L'Escale to
drop me off for another night in the stainless steel
room to wait for the grey van to bring me even
farther north the next morning.

Queen

Cat Eyes and Miss Calvin Klein, both of whom I had met in Le Village, were already in Bailie Cottage when I got to the Farm. Other girls I had met in other Ville Marie placements were there too, but the atmosphere of Bailie was totally different than most of the places I'd already been in.

The days were much more structured, right from the moment you woke up, till they locked you in your room at night. In fact, a lot of times being locked in my room was a total relief from being continuously observed. It was like I could let my wall down and escape into sleep or the glorious world of books.

There were more therapy sessions and group meetings than I had experienced in other placements. These were long emotionally draining affairs if you weren't bored to tears. Often they were repetitive and monotonous. I grew to loathe the group meetings.

We never left the unit not even to go to the gym. We did all our physical activities in the common room and attended classes upstairs in the same building. We could and would easily be sent

127

to our rooms for the smallest of infractions.
Sometimes for just having the wrong look on your
face.   Sometimes having a temper tantrum was the
only way to get a little time to yourself. It felt good
to vent and curse and slam your door so they could
lock it behind you.

The cutlery was counted before and after
each meal, and if one went missing, we would all be
locked down till it was located. I remember
spending many hours in our rooms one day because
a tablespoon went missing. Someone was in danger
of being gagged or digging a tunnel, I guess.
Thankfully it was finally found in a bowl in the
fridge.

The whole time I was there, I felt like I was
constantly on edge, just waiting for the guillotine to
drop.

In Le Village, friendships between the girls
were tolerated, if not encouraged. But that was not
the case in Bailie. It seemed to me that getting too
close to another girl in the unit put you at great risk.
The implication was that it was detrimental to your
treatment, so the girls seemed to keep a distance
between them. We tried not to talk to each other in
front of staff for fear of being accused of plotting
some nefarious scheme, or of being a lesbian. It was
a totally isolating feeling. I felt alone and very
depressed there. I was anxious and scared most of
the time. The closeness I had felt to some of the
girls in Le Village had evaporated. I was very
lonely.

Slave to the Farm

I was in Bailie waiting for a bed in Renaissance, so at least there was some light at the end of my tunnel, but the days remained brutally long and the nights were no better. As if I needed more reasons to dislike Bailie, I was spooked by my roommate, China Doll. She was there for murder and was the second teen murderer I met in the system. I met Miss Calvin Klein in Village first, but they were very different. I liked Miss Klein.

I met China Doll in Bailie, and knew nothing of her story before I'd gotten there. Miss Calvin Klein's story on the other hand was all over the news; however, I never saw any coverage of it. Miss Calvin Klein's story was fodder for many rumors in the system long before I met her. While in Le Village, I knew only that she was there because she had killed her sister and attacked her father. The details were not something we talked openly about.

She came from an influential family in Montreal, and had been a teenage model for, guess who, Calvin Klein. She was very tall, very beautiful and very quiet. I liked her, but many of the girls thought she was a liar.

It wasn't until Bailie, though, that I learned the details of what she had done. Even with those details to me she somehow seemed like a victim. I felt bad for her, but I reminded myself she was a murderer and so did the other girls in the unit. The general consensus was that she was lying about what really happened and that she shouldn't be trusted.

During a group therapy session in Bailie, she was asked by one of the girls to tell us about that fateful day.

"What really happened?" she asked.

This is the story she told, as I remember it: both she and her sister had been adopted by their parents as babies. Her sister was a couple of years older and adopted a few years before Miss Klein. She described her relationship with her sister as strained, and not at all loving. She said they fought physically all their lives or as long as she could remember.

Miss Klein said it got noticeably worse when she started modeling as a young teen. She said her older sister was jealous of her immediate success in the fashion industry. Big Sis, a nurse I think, was short and fat and just not cut out for a life on the runway, Miss Klein told us.

Their parents had some public acclaim of their own. Mrs. Klein wrote for the Montreal Gazette while Mr. Klein was in law I think. They were very proud of Miss Klein's budding career.

Miss Klein said that the day it happened she was getting ready for a ski trip, and was at home alone, packing her bags. She said she planned on taking her sister's K-Way pants* without permission, and was in her sister's bedroom when Big Sis came home early and found her there looking for them. They started to argue and it eventually turned violent.

Miss Klein said there was something very different about this fight. Sis was overly angry, she said. The fight seemed much more serious than previous ones. Sis was screaming that she was going to kill her and that she hated her. Big Sis screamed she wished Miss Klein was dead.

In the course of the fight, while Sis had the upper hand and was on top, she wrapped her hands around Miss Klein's neck and started to strangle her. Miss Klein said she thought she was going to black out or worse, die. She was gasping for air and in a panic reached her arms above her head to grab whatever was in reach. She found a phone cord there. She swung the cord forward with both hands and caught her sister under the chin. It was never really clear to us if Miss Klein had broken Sis's neck or actually wrapped the cord around her neck and strangled her to death, but what happened next was what assured Miss Klein would receive the maximum sentence possible under the Youth Offenders Act:* three years.

She said when she realized she had killed her sister, she panicked. She said she sat staring at the body, not knowing what to do. She said it was as if she was watching from the corner of the room as she dragged her sister's body and stuffed it under her bed.

Next, she just finished packing and headed for the garage to get her skis. While there, her father came home and drove into the garage. She said she had no memory of attacking her father, but believe she did it because she was afraid he would find the body before she could get away.

The girls sat transfixed and silent. To me it seemed surreal or like it was a TV show. I just couldn't see this crying, regret-filled little girl as a murderer. It didn't seem possible that the family that came and saw Miss Klein every week could be the same family we had just heard about. I could see Mr. Klein there in my mind's eye, hugging and kissing his daughter. I wasn't sure if I should be afraid of her. My experience of her was of a kind, shy teenager who wasn't much different than me. In fact, Scarecrow called her a 'poor little rich kid' too.

After sharing her story with us, the girls in Bailie started avoiding her, and for weeks afterwards, Miss. Klein walked around with her eyes cast to the floor. The weight of the world visible on her shoulders. I felt sorry for her, but kept my distance.

In stark contrast to my feelings about Miss Klein were my feelings about China Doll. My feelings for my roommate were anything but charitable. China Doll was in Bailie serving her year long sentence for shooting her father through the face as he lay sleeping next to her mother.

She was from out east, New Brunswick I think, but I was never really certain why she was brought all the way to Montreal to do her time. She creeped me out from the first moment I laid eyes on her. She was very, very quiet, and rarely said anything. She seemed withdrawn, and her eyes were always a trillion miles away. Her skin had this translucent quality to it that allowed you to see all the blue veins flowing beneath. She was so powdery white it made her look like... well, a china doll. She had these perfectly round red spots on her cheeks that looked like they had been painted there by the doll maker who had lovingly made her.

She was never asked while I was there to share her story with the group, but at night, while locked in our room together, I got pieces of the story from her.

She told me her father was an alcoholic who beat her, her siblings and mother regularly. She said they were all very afraid of him and his mood swings. Her mother was most often the target of her father's rage, but her and her brother got more than their share. She said she felt powerless and wanted to protect her mother from him. She believed her father would one day kill her mother or brother if someone didn't do something. China Doll told me she often thought about killing him before she finally put a bullet in him.

She said she never regretted the murder for a second. He deserved to die for what he did to them, she told me. She had absolutely no grief or remorse. It seemed to me that she had no feelings at all about what had happened. She was disconnected from it. She talked about it like it was a story she had heard from someone else.

133

Slave to the Farm

China Doll said the night she killed her father was just like any other. After work, her father came home and started drinking. By the time dinner was served, he was drunk. He demanded all of her mother's money to go to the bar. She didn't have much, so he hit her, and told the kids they better find some more or he would get even angrier. China Doll gave him the last seventeen dollars she had saved in her piggy bank, and the whole family was relieved to see him go out.

Everyone was in bed when he stumbled through the door a couple of hours later. China Doll woke up when he came in. Then as usual, she heard her parents start arguing in their bedroom. That is when she decided she was going to shoot him. She had witnessed this routine many times before. Her father was going to rape her mother before finally passing out. She said she knew it would never end.

When it quieted down, China Doll got out of bed and crept downstairs to get the hand gun her father kept in a drawer in the kitchen. She said she had to look for the bullets because they were not with the gun. Finally, she found them and loaded the weapon. She creeped upstairs and quietly slipped into her parents' room. She said she watched them sleeping for a little while, and almost changed her mind. But her father rolled over onto his back; making her afraid he might wake up and find her there. She tip-toed over to his side of the bed, pointed the gun at his head, and pulled the trigger. She got the minimum sentence of one year.

Slave to the Farm

I never felt safe falling asleep before her, often waiting for her soft snoring sounds to come before I could even begin to think about sleeping myself.

Early one morning just before sunrise, I woke up feeling the hair standing up on the back of my neck. I felt like I was being watched. I rolled over to see China Doll standing next to my bed with a vacant stare in her eyes. Just standing there, looking like a ghost hugging a pillow. She didn't seem to notice I was awake till I said something to her.

"What the fuck are you doing?" I said, waking her out of her reverie.

She seemed to come back to herself, and looked around confused. She didn't answer me, but just stood there staring around the room, definitely more present than she had been seconds earlier. It seemed like she was surprised to see me there. I sat up and looked around the room. Her bed had been made with military precision, and she was fully dressed. Her side of the room had been arranged perfectly, and not a single thing was out of place. Something was very strange in her demeanor, but I couldn't place a finger on what. I was filled with anxiety; my stomach clenched so hard it hurt.

It was barely light in the room, but it was obvious she had been up for quite a while. How long she had been standing next to my bed with a pillow in her hands is anyone's guess. Why she was standing there is something I don't like to reflect on.

Slave to the Farm

I jumped out of bed, went straight to the locked door, and started banging on it. It was too early for the day staff to have arrived yet, so the night watchman came to the window in the door.

"Let me out of here now!" I begged him through the door.

He started to resist but something in my eyes registered with him. I saw his face change. He saw my fear, and I recognized his concern. He unlocked the door and let me out. I ran past him to the washroom.

I spent so long in the washroom splashing cold water on my face and staring into my own eyes, that he came to the door and asked if I was all right. I called out that all was good, then giving myself one last splash, I came out. I asked him how long before the day staff got there, and he told me he had about an hour to go. I had calmed down considerably, and was ready to go back to my room knowing he wasn't allowed to let me out other than to go to the washroom, so I took a deep breath and followed him back.

China Doll was lying on her made bed. She looked up at me but didn't sit up. I just went to my own bed and sat down. I sat staring at her back till I heard the morning staff entering the building. I got up, got dressed, made my bed, then went to stand at the window in the door. The watchman must have told the staff about letting me out earlier, and that he suspected something was amiss. Before too long there was a staff member at my window surprised to see me there on the other side waiting for him. He unlocked the door and came into our room.

"Wow, you are both up, dressed and have your beds made. What's the occasion?" he asked looking at me, but I just shrugged my shoulders.

China Doll said nothing, looking up from her bed. He stood there glancing back and forth between us, not really knowing what to say, but knowing something was not right. There was a charged energy between us. We all stood in uncomfortable silence.

"Well Erika, seeing you are ready, why don't you go set the table for breakfast and see if there is anything else that needs doing." Gratefully, I left the room and headed for the kitchen.

Later that day, I asked for another roommate, and by that evening I was gladly bunking with Cat Eyes like old times.

I wasn't pressed by the staff to explain what happened that morning. I just said I had a nightmare, but when I asked and then pleaded for another roommate, they wanted some more concrete reasons. I didn't have any concrete reasons, I said. I just didn't trust her. I thought she was weird, I said. I couldn't bring myself to say I was scared of her, but I implied it.

The staff thought I was being over dramatic. What they couldn't ignore was the intensity of my concerns, or the atmosphere that was obvious that morning. They finally agreed, and I was moved into another room.

Slave to the Farm

China Doll didn't get a new roommate.

Me and Bobbie McGee

Janis Joplin

Happy times, the discussion of moving me from Bailie to Renaissance was initiated. My primary worker* from Renaissance began visiting me.

Mrs. Beasley was a quiet, gentle woman with soft hands and a soft voice, which housed a little girl laugh. She reminded me of a favorite toy I had as a child called a Mrs. Beasley doll.

I liked her and enjoyed spending time with her. She liked my poetry and often asked me to write for her. Beasley would give me a list of words like rage, angel, snow, pain, and I would have to write poems about each. I didn't see how it would help her, but I loved doing it.

She gave me a reading list on many different topics, but the one book I remember most was on sexual abuse, molestation, and incest.

139

Slave to the Farm

A few months earlier while in Le Village, all the girls were rounded up and deposited into the common room to watch a documentary on molestation. During that fateful viewing I had an epiphany about the rape I had experienced a month before my fourteenth birthday.

It was the first time I called it rape in my mind. It was the first time I considered forgiving myself for what happened, and it was the first time I considered that maybe it wasn't totally my fault. When Beasley gave me the book months later, it resonated with me on a deep level, one I had never explored before.

I don't want to imply that there was some explosive therapeutic cleansing of my subconscious. It was more like a slow steady drip finding a crack in my armour. The feelings of anger, hatred, fear and self-loathing that the authors of those stories in the book expressed mirrored my own feelings. They felt dirty and unloved. So did I. Their behaviors and social problems were recognizable in my own life. I found myself wondering if I should tell someone about what had happened to me. I thought about it, but didn't.

Finally, the day of the move dawned, and Beasley came over around noon to collect me and my stuff. We walked across the campus with everything I owned in a garbage bag. She showed me to my room, and left me to unpack and settle in.

Slave to the Farm

It was a weekday, and all the other girls were at the school building. Beasley showed me around the whole cottage: the common room, kitchen, office, and then downstairs where the visiting room was, along with the shower room. We would be allowed to shower privately here. What a bonus.

The girls finally filed in after school. As Lizard burst through the door, I was there to meet her. We were ecstatic to see each other again and immediately fell back into our comfortable camaraderie.

She still had our on-going rummy scores from Le Village, and we just picked up where we left off. I thought, this time I'm really going to make this work.

In Renaissance we would be allowed to have our own cigarettes. We were issued two packs for the week, and expected to make them last. It seemed like a good deal, until you did the math. We were actually losing a cigarette a day from the Le Village standard of eight, but gained one from Bailie's standard of six.

I was popular that day, because Beasley gave me both of my packs of smokes, and many of the girls were out of cigarettes already. Negotiations for mine started almost immediately. By handing out smokes that day, I gained a whole pack from the other girls. Before too long, Lizard and I were in the cigarette business.

Slave to the Farm

Some of the girls were able to buy cigarettes of their own, but they were not allowed to bring those back to the unit. They were handed in at the office, and held till the next outing or weekend visits home.

Many of us who had been there for the cigarette coup in Le Village started plotting the next one to take place right there in Renaissance. This time we were booking for the right to have our own cigarettes whenever we wanted them. We argued that they were our property, and that if we had bought them, or were given them, we should have the right to them.

Meeting after meeting, we would bring it up, pointing out that the boys were allowed their own cigarettes, and demanding to know why there was a double standard. We told them there were other double standards that we were aware of, too. Like the strict dress restrictions placed on the girls: we weren't allowed to wear jeans to school, but that was all the boys wore. We argued the boys had a lot more private time to use the gym for sports or weights, and the skating rink for games of one on one. Even the swimming pool during the summer was more accessible to them we said. The girls weren't entitled to those privileges without being chaperoned. The older boys also got many more opportunities to work off The Farm. It got them work experience, pocket money and cigarettes, we pointed out.

Slave to the Farm

We cried foul, and eventually wore the decision-makers down till they agreed to allow us access to our own cigarettes and raised our allowance to three packs a week.

I fell into the routine of Renaissance easily. I started going to the school in the building next to Beaton with all the rest of the girls. On the Farm the boys outnumbered the girls about five to one. Needless to say, the new girls got a lot of attention whether we wanted it or not. It certainly wasn't like any other high school. The classes were small, sometimes only having 3 or 4 students per teacher. We did all the core subjects such as math, English, science and French, but I remember the classes being mixed and not really separated into grades. Math was my favourite course at Shawbridge High School. English Pete taught us out of this tiny blue hard-covered algebra book that he told us he used when he was in high school. The math I did learn came from him.

Not long after getting to Renaissance, I started hanging out with a boy from the West Island. We hadn't met before Shawbridge, but at home we knew some of the same people. I guess that's why we gave it a try. We really didn't get along that well. He was broody, quiet, and always had an intense concentrated look on his face.

Rumblefish was in L'Avinir cottage. We used to walk together around the oval driveway that our cottages looked out onto. He never really had much to say. We would walk in uncomfortable silence till one of us got called into our cottage. It didn't take too long before another guy from Rumblefish's cottage started joining us, and he and I would chat and giggle, and finally Rumblefish would just not come at all.

Moose would always be there, waiting to take a walk when I showed up. He gave me many Harley Davidson t-shirts, and I could be found wearing them any chance I got. He got jealous if any other guys talked to me, so I avoided the argument by just staying away from the other guys as much as possible. We became inseparable.

Moose was from Verdun. He didn't talk about his family to me, or why he was in Shawbridge, but I found him sweet and charming. He was really funny sometimes, and I thought I was in love. Sometimes we would sneak a kiss or hold hands till some staff would put a stop to it.

Also in L'Avinir was a wiry native guy named Mac. The three of us would walk the circle sometimes. Moose kept telling me I should get one of the other girls to come with us so Mac wouldn't be lonely, so one day I convinced Missy to come along with us. Pretty soon we were a team, and would eventually all AWOL together.

Almost as soon as I got to Renaissance, I joined the church choir Beasley organized. It meant going to church services every Sunday to sing the songs, but that was a small price to pay for the chance to sing with the group. We met one night a week to practice and learn new songs.

Lizard and I went together, and we sang most of the harmonies for the choir. The Shawbridge choir got to go on field trips, and perform for visitors, schools, churches and community groups.

Being in the choir was by far the most enriching activity I did during that time period. It certainly gave me an outlet for some of my pent up frustration, and built some much needed self-confidence in me. It felt great to get complements for something that came easy to me, and it felt really rewarding to be working in a group.

Beasley would often tell me she could tell how I was feeling by how much effort I put into the choir.

One night during choir practice, Beasley told us about a talent show that was being organized in the gym. She was looking for acts. The hope was that at least someone from every cottage would offer up some of their talent. She told us we could perform as a choir, but that it would be better if we tried solo acts. She looked at me expectantly.

At first, I thought, no way was I going to get up and sing alone. But she worked on me till I agreed to sing a song. I chose *The Rose* by Bette Midler. I liked the song because I had heard it was written about Janis Joplin. People always told me I looked like Janis, so I thought; I'll dress up in my best Joplin costume and belt out a song about her.

Slave to the Farm

The show was put together quickly, so the acts didn't get a whole lot of time to practice. Padre, the minister who delivered the services on Sunday, agreed to play guitar for me. I think we practiced the song twice an hour before we were supposed to go on stage.

I felt sick to my stomach and unprepared. I was the fourth act to go on, and sat in the audience watching the show with Moose, Mac, and Missy till Miss Calvin Klein started her act, then made my way back stage.

Padre stood with me, offering words of encouragement and telling me I would be great. He told me not to look at the people, but above their heads. He played me a note to find the key, and finally the applause at the end of Miss Klein's dance act signaled my kick at the can.

A mic was placed in the middle of the stage and Padre and I made our entrance heading for it. I had sung in front of many people before, in the smoking pit at school, in Le Village's common room and with the choir, but at that moment looking out at the sea of expectant faces, I suddenly felt like I had lead shoes on. It took longer to walk to the mic than I intended. Padre urged me forward and whispered to take a deep breath.

There were all these people in the gym, sitting there looking at me dressed in a silly costume. I felt naked. Padre started playing and had to do the intro twice before I had the nerve to sing the first note. As I sung that first line a silence fell over the crowd. All I could hear was the nervousness in my voice, a slight tremble. I started to gain confidence as the song moved along, and hit my stride by the first chorus. The guitar strummed along, and just as I was about to start the third and final verse, someone called out from the hushed audience. It threw me off and I missed my cue and stepped back from the microphone. Padre just kept playing and encouraging me to the mic again. I stepped forward, closed my eyes, and finished the song.

There was a slight delay before the audience bust into loud applause. My eyes flew open, and I looked at the throng for the first time. I was filled with this warm fuzzy feeling radiating out of my stomach, bleeding into my whole body. I had never felt anything like it before. I stood there a second, took a bow then walked off stage in a daze.

Since that day I have often felt the bowel-liquefying reality check of stage fright, as well as the warm satisfied afterglow of applause, but never as acutely as I did before and after that performance. It's one of those moments that make you smile as you gaze back at it.

When the show was over, and we were all walking back to our cottages, Fryer Tuck, another guy I knew from the West Island, who was in Springfield, came up to me and said, "Way to go, Erika! Wow! All those times I played guitar at Fairview Shopping centre, how come you never sang with me? I mean, till today, I didn't even know you could sing."

I just smiled at him and said, "Neither did I."

Twenty-two years later, I interviewed Fryer Tuck about his experience on The Farm. He gave me the compliment of remembering that day, and offered me one of my most candid interviews.

You Could Have Been A Lady

April Wine

After a few months in Renaissance, I had earned the privilege of a weekend visit home. I had already had a couple of day passes over those months, but I was to have two whole nights in my own bed, and three lazy days to lounge around my own house. It had been over a year since I had been home for the night, and I was looking forward to it with eager anticipation.

After school on Friday, I rushed back to the cottage and packed my weekend bag. The Shawbridge van would be there after dinner to pick up all the kids on The Farm with weekend privileges, and drive them to a metro in Montreal.

My mother was at the metro to meet the van, and we drove highway 20 back to Beaconsfield. My younger brother was bubbling with excitement at having me home for the weekend, but my older brother was predictably absent from my homecoming. My dad had his own apartment in St. Laurent, and would see me the following day.

It felt awkward in the house. I felt like a visitor, and like my very presence upset the delicate balance that had been reached since mine and my father's departure. I already knew that I wouldn't be allowed out to visit friends, and I didn't want to blow the chance of being able to come again, so I was on my best behaviour.

After throwing my bag into a bedroom that no longer felt like mine, I went back down to hang out with my younger brother. I knew he missed me terribly while I was gone, and he had changed a lot from the last time we got to be alone together. He didn't seem like such a little kid anymore. Two of his buddies crashed through the door as I came down.

"Let's walk down to Pinto's and rent a movie," suggested Bocca.

I wasn't sure if my mom was going to let me out with the boys to walk the couple of blocks to the neighbourhood strip mall. I sent my brother to beg for me. She agreed, and the four of us headed out.

As we rounded the first corner, we all broke out cigarettes and lit up. While smoking our butts, my brother handed me something and asked, "Is this real?"

I looked at the rolled spliff he gave me, and brought it up to my nose to take a sniff.

"It sure is! Give me a light," I said, tossing my butt away and sticking the spliff in my mouth.

Slave to the Farm

"No way, I'm going to sell it." he argued.

"You can't sell a rolled spliff," I scoffed at him. But the three amigos assured me that, yes, they could buy rolled joints at school for five bucks each.

"Come on you guys, you're not going to give me the first spliff I've seen in months and not let me smoke it, are you? Give me a light!"

Finally, my brother conceded and gave me the lighter. I fired it up and we stood in a circle and passed the hash around among us. It was the first time I ever did drugs with my brother or any of his friends. Before that, they all seemed too young, but something had changed. We all got super stoned on the smoke and rented Jimi Hendrix's *"Live at Monterrey"*.

Mom had gone up to her room to read before bed, so she didn't see our bloodshot eyes or smell the dope on us. However, she was satisfied that we ALL made it back. She turned off her light and went to bed.

After making popcorn and cracking open cans of pop, we settled down in the family room and watched the concert. My brother had never heard of Jimi Hendrix. He enjoyed the movie so much we rewound it and watched it again as soon as it was over. He became an enthusiastic Hendrix fan from that day forward.

The next day, I slept in till noon and spent the day reading, talking on the phone, and watching TV. Scott's friends came over after dinner and we

151

played cards till well after midnight. We liked to play Cribbage, Downtown, or Asshole.

Sunday morning was much the same, except that I had to be downtown to meet the van transporting me back to The Farm at 6 pm.

Sometime in the afternoon, I found a hair-streaking kit while snooping in the bathroom cabinet, and asked my mom about it. She offered to streak my hair for me. We had never done anything like that before. I couldn't remember my mother brushing or styling my hair since I was very little. I happily agreed.

She had never used the product before. You had to put the cap on, and then pull pieces of your hair through the tiny holes with what looked like a crochet needle. You could pull as much or as little hair through to achieve the desired level of colouring. We were both inexperienced, so Mom pulled much more hair through the cap than needed. It was afternoon when we started, and as the time to meet the bus grew closer, we began to rush. Mom put the chemicals on my head. The instructions said to wait twenty minutes, then check to see if the colour was right. After no more than five minutes, I noticed that my hair was rapidly getting lighter. At eight minutes my hair looked white under the clear plastic bag over my head. I started to worry.

"Mom, maybe I should wash this off?" I screamed from the bathroom mirror.

Slave to the Farm

"Well, the instructions said to wait twenty minutes." She called back from the kitchen, where she was fixing a hasty dinner before we left.

I came out of the bathroom to show her how much the chemicals had bleached my hair blond already. She was shocked. We agreed that I should wash out the dye before the twenty minutes was up. I went upstairs to use the detachable shower head. I washed out the dye and conditioned my hair. When I stood up to see how it looked, my mouth dropped open. It was shocking blond. I blew dried my hair and again stood looking at the dramatic change.

I actually liked it. Some of my auburn hair was still visible, but because we had pulled so much hair through the cap, most of my hair was very blond. I walked downstairs to show my mother our handiwork, and thought to myself, 'Am I ever glad she did this to me, or else she would have been pissed off'.

She was shocked, but there was no time to do anything about it. We ate our meal and rushed out to meet the van at the metro downtown.

All the clients in all the cottages on the Farm were assigned primary workers. These primaries acted like social workers or advocates for the individual kids on the Farm. Your Shawbridge primary would communicate directly with the Director of Youth Protection at Ville Marie Social Services, (AKA Head Honcho) or your social worker, and/or parents about your individual needs.

Slave to the Farm

I actually liked living in Renaissance. It was much better than Le Village, and infinitely better than Bailey cottage. Beasley was wonderful to have as my primary in Renaissance. I felt like we were friends, and I enjoyed her company. She liked to take the kids into town, but I didn't often get to go: I was too much of an AWOL risk. But she'd often bring me back little things to let me know she was thinking about me. I liked her as my worker, and I liked her as a staff. She was fair and negotiable. The atmosphere in the cottage was pretty good too. There was a kind of bond forged among all the girls in the cottage. Few major personality conflicts were insurmountable, and the social benefits of living on a co-ed campus were very important to all us blooming teenagers.

We played sports and had lots of books to read. We were given some free time, and the weekends home were like icing on the cake. I did pretty well in Renaissance, and although I thought about running away every so often, it was mostly when I wanted to attend a party or a concert or some other event. I dreamed of running to go to those things, but I never did while I was home on any weekends.

One weekend however, I did leave my mother's house and not return. I was on the run for about six weeks and it was all because Moose came to see me when we were both on a weekend pass.

He came to my house one Saturday night while I was playing cards in the basement with my brother and his friends. My mother let him in not knowing he was from The Farm. He sat with us for a while trying to impress the guys with his crime exploits, and mentioned he had a gun with him that he had hidden in the park down the street. The guys wanted to see it. We told my mother we were going to rent a movie and headed out.

It was a sawed off-shotgun. The gang was impressed by it, but I didn't like it at all. I kept thinking about what happened with Diz. I wanted him to put it away before we all got in trouble. I wasn't worried about someone getting hurt. I was well-insulated with teen-age feelings of immortality, but I knew that if any of the neighbours saw us with it, the cops wouldn't be far behind. Moose slipped the gun into the pocket of his oversized coat, and the gang suggested we go back to play video games.

Moose and I told them to go ahead, and leave us at the park so we could have some privacy. My brother reluctantly agreed to meet me later at home, but I never made it. It would be just another time I let my little brother down.

Slave to the Farm

Fleetwood Mac

Moose and I took the 206 bus from Windermere to the MacDonald's on St Charles Boulevard, then caught the 211 to the Atwater Metro station.

There was no real reason for me to run away. I actually was doing really well at the time, but I was impulsive and unsure of myself. I wanted to be liked, and that meant going along with bad decisions, listening to selfish people who didn't have my wellbeing at heart, and participating in suicidal stunts of stupidity.

I still ask myself what was going on inside of me at those times, but I don't have answers. There is this deep bottomless abyss of questions. I search my psyche for the triggers that sent me off down the rabbit hole, but still nothing. I'm left only with a sense of hopelessness and self-loathing. I was crippled by self-loathing. I hated everything about myself: my hair, my body, my face. I was nerdy, and weak. I was a crybaby and a whiner. I felt like I couldn't do anything right. They don't put good kids in jail for being good or lovable or trustworthy. Any popular image of an all-around good Canadian kid shows them smiling and happy, not sullen and depressed. Bad kids are violent druggies and assigned to special programs because they are stupid. We weren't worth loving. We couldn't be trusted and we certainly couldn't trust.

It was so hard to do the right thing when all the messages were that something was wrong with me, that I was bad inside. All of my internal dialogue was negative, peppered with thoughts of suicide. Even though I was doing well at Renaissance, I didn't feel good, emotionally, socially, or spiritually. I felt like a fraud. I was so fucking angry, but I couldn't express that anger in any satisfying acceptable way. Frustration was a constant companion that didn't clean up after itself, so my life was one big angry mess. No surprise I found myself in messy situations. This AWOL turned into one of the messiest.

Moose and I hopped the metro down to St. Laurent to a flea-bitten motel, where we met up with Mac and Missy. We hung out in a room overlooking the hookers below. We smoked hash and cigarettes. We ate fast food, and Mac soaked the cast off his broken arm in the sink.

Later we had sex, Moose and I in one bed, Missy and Mac in the other. It was awkward and embarrassing. I had never had sex in front of other people and even though M&M weren't paying any attention to us, I just couldn't get into it. Moose finally gave up trying. We lay there listening to the noises from the other bed.

The next day, we hung out downtown on the streets of Montreal and later in the afternoon, Mac and Missy said they wanted to go meet the van back to The Farm. We parted ways and Moose and I headed to Verdun. He brought me to his friends' apartment and they let us stay with them for a couple of days.

The next couple of weeks with Moose were some of my darkest. The shadow of that time weighs heavy in my memories. I witnessed a number of crimes committed in those fateful weeks: B&E, drug dealing, car theft, fraud, assault, and robbery.

Within hours of getting to Verdun, Moose had fronted some dope and started dealing. He had grown up there and everywhere we went he knew people. He sold all the dope he had and bought some more. We did drugs too, but we didn't eat much and I lost weight.

One evening, while we were doing the rounds, we met up with three guys. Moose started negotiations for the pills these guys had for sale. I'm not sure what they were, but the Three Amigos talked them up like they were gold. Moose got a handful and off we went. We did some more walking around, sold some of the pills, then met up with a longtime friend and associate of Moose's named Prickles.

Slave to the Farm

Moose hadn't seen Prickles in months. As the old friends reconnected, I sat around waiting in the park outside Verdun metro. I noticed a group of four girls on the other side of the park while Moose was deep in conversation with Prickles. The girls seemed to be talking about us, and their sleazy demeanor made me leery of them. As soon as I got a chance, I was going to point them out to Moose, but he left in a hurry with Prickles telling me over his shoulder they'd be back in a half hour.

As I watched the guys saunter up the street, a feeling of foreboding reached up and grabbed me by the throat. I swung my gaze back around to look at the foursome, but they weren't where I'd last seen them. I got up from the bench, planning to go to the depeneur* and get something to eat with the little bit of change I had in my pocket, but before I could make it around the building I came face to face with the foursome.

"Where you going in such a hurry, Sweet Cheeks? We want to talk to you."

I didn't really know what to say. I didn't know who they were or what they wanted. I assumed they were going to rob me, but I had nothing to steal. I wasn't even carrying a purse, which I would have gladly handed over.

"I've got nothing to steal." I told her, working hard to keep the fear percolating in my body out of my voice, and tried to push past her. She stepped into my path and shoved me back with a blast to my chest. I stumbled backwards, but regained my balance before I fell.

"What the fuck do you want?" I barked at her.

"You think you can just keep fucking my boyfriend and I'm not gonna notice?" She screamed, inches from my face. The three girls behind her fanned out in a semi-circle around me.

"What the fuck are you talking about? What boyfriend? I don't need your ol' man, I got my own."

"Moose was my ol' man long before you... whore. And now I'm gonna kick your ass, just so you remember."

She charged at me with her fists balled. Her first punch just missed the side of my head, and clipped my ear, leaving it stinging and hot. Again I stumbled backwards only this time I landed flat on my ass. I didn't have time to get back up again before the four of them surrounded me, and started punching and kicking. I balled up on the ground and tried to protect my head, so the four of them just dragged me around on the pavement kicking at me.

I don't remember any pain. The fear produced a painkiller that made their pummeling somewhat ineffectual. I don't know what chased them off, but eventually I realized I was alone. The kicking and dragging had stopped. I sat up and looked around.

There was an older couple watching me from across the park. I wasn't sure if they had

161

witnessed the fight or just happened to see me laying there. The man seemed concerned, and made moves in my direction, but his wife pulled on his arm, pleading with him to mind his own business. I kind of waved them off to let them know I was ok, and they hurried away down the street.

I got up to my feet, and start looking for injuries. The posse had ripped the sleeve of my shirt, and my left arm was bleeding from being scrapped on the pavement. Both knees of my faded jeans had worn away exposing scrapped bleeding legs. My left ear and the side of my face were tender from the couple of punches that made contact, and my ribs were sore from being kicked. All in all, I was battered but not really hurt.

Just as I was coming around the corner of the metro, I ran into Moose. He did a double take at my condition.

"Holy shit. What happened?"

"Your girlfriend just gave me a courtesy call. You could have warned me about her. There was four of them, you know," I croaked at him, holding back tears.

"My girlfriend? Which one? What did she look like?"

I described the posse to him, and particularly the sheriff of the group. Moose started laughing, figuring out who the group of girls were.

"Ah, she's such a bitch. I went out with her over a year ago. She keeps writing me on The Farm. She keeps telling me she loves me, and when I get out she wants me to come live with her, and her mother. Don't worry, she's just a slut. I saw her earlier when I went to the store, and she must have followed me to the park. I'm sorry, but you look like you're not that badly hurt. We just need to get you cleaned up and you'll be OK. Taking on four girls... I'm proud of you. Prickles has a place just a couple of blocks over. Let's go have a drink."

I was really shaken up, but Moose's blasé attitude about being jumped wasn't really sympathetic, so I just suffered in silence and followed Moose to Prickles' apartment.

In the years since that beating, I've often wondered if he had set me up. If he left the park so the fight could take place. Maybe as a hazing* exercise. I never saw the girls again anywhere in Verdun. Moose and I never spoke of it but I became afraid to go anywhere alone without him.

Prickles lived with his girlfriend, Granny, and another roommate named Sparrow. Sparrow was a private guy, who had a private closet of a room in the large apartment. I rarely saw him because he was the only one who worked, and when he wasn't at his job, he spent most of his time in his room. When I did see him, we got along well, and I really liked him. We often talked about books. He lent me a couple while I was there, including To Kill A Mocking Bird and The Catcher In The Rye.

Moose and I stayed at the apartment for a couple of weeks while Granny nursed me back to health. She had powerful painkillers that she was

163

prescribed for a chronic back condition, and she would sometimes share these with me. We would then spend hours together in an opiate-induced daze on the couch.

Meanwhile, Moose and Prickles went on a crime spree. They sold drugs from the apartment till late afternoon, and then head out till late at night. They never returned empty-handed. They were doing B&Es and robberies, and of course, dealing drugs.

They brought the stolen stuff they didn't want to pawn and the food they stole out of freezers to the apartment. Granny and I would cook up whatever food there was and everyone would gorge.

One night, they brought home a turkey dinner and all the fixings, so we popped it into the oven at 11:45 pm and had a full turkey dinner at 5 am.

I got three tattoos in the couple of weeks I lived in that apartment. One of the crowd that hung out there regularly to buy drugs, had a homemade tattoo gun. He inked a Led Zeppelin Swan Song on my left breast, and some small flowers on my right. They weren't my first tattoos. I got a small symbol on my ankle when I ran away to Sudbury with Chunk, but these were much bigger than that first one.

The third tattoo was a unicorn on my right butt cheek. For whatever reason, that tattoo hurt the most. I was in so much pain I couldn't really hold still or pay attention. When the tattoo was done, I

twisted my body to look at it. Picasso had added
Moose's name under it. I freaked out and had a fit,
yelling and screaming while all those present
laughed at me.

"Well, it's on there for good now" cackled
Picasso.

I never let him near me again. Moose
thought it was funny, too. Seems I'm the only one
who didn't get the joke.

It was ten years before I got that name
covered. I think of that occasion as the first day of
my new life. Getting the new ink tweaked my self-
esteem, and a new and improved me was born.

It took ten more years till I covered the two
tattoos on my chest, joining them into one image. It
was the cheapest and most effective psychotherapy
I've ever had. I left that tattoo parlor with a lighter
wallet, but banking much more confidence than I
had when I went in.

Slave to the Farm

BAD COMPANY

BAD COMPANY

Prickles had developed this noticeable hatred for me. He disagreed with everything I said, ordered me around, and told me to shut up as often as he could. He kept telling me that the only reason I was allowed to stay was because of Moose. He wasn't shy about berating me in front of Moose, but it often led to an argument between them, so he would save his venom for those rare moments when Moose wasn't around to defend me.

Granny would try to protect me too, but she was afraid of Prickles. She didn't want to incite him either. She tried to distract him when Moose wasn't around.

One night, Prickles brought home a shotgun. I was sure it was a bad omen. It was a crude dangerous looking thing with the barrel sawed off, and I was always glad when it was hiding under Granny's bed and not being handled. It reminded me of the one Moose brought to the park and I wondered what had happened to that one. Moose

167

and Prickles didn't bring it out with them most of the time, but sometimes they would. I suspected they had graduated to armed robberies, but never confirmed it. They took it one evening, and left with it tucked into the inside pocket of Moose's coat.

Granny and I settled in to watch TV, expecting the guys to be out all night. The boys returned an hour and a half later. They had scored some more of the pills Moose had the day of the fight, and we all decided to try them.

I dropped two of them first, then another two about twenty minutes later. I blacked out. I don't really remember much about what happened after I took those second two pills but I do remember waking up in the back seat of a strange car. The time on the clock in the front showed 1:30 am. I was alone, and parked outside a large house. My eyes were rolling in my head, and I had a hard time sitting up. I couldn't really focus without a lot of effort, and even struggled to keep my eyes open. Eventually, I lost the battle and lay back down on the back seat.

It was light the next time I opened my eyes. Again I didn't recognize where I was, and again I was alone. This time though, I was in a bed in an unfamiliar room. I was fully dressed and could hear a mumble of voices coming from the other side of the door. None seemed familiar to me.

Slave to the Farm

My bladder was beyond full. I was filled with apprehension about what I would find on the other side of the door, so I crept up and listened for at least one voice I could identify. No luck. I couldn't put a name or face to any of them.

It actually sounded like a family having dinner. Yes, I could definitely hear a child's voice. It gave me confidence to open the door slowly.

Everyone stopped talking as soon as I cracked the door open a sliver. Finally, I had it fully opened, and the moment of truth was upon me. I stepped out into the kitchen. As I had suspected, a family was sitting at the table eating dinner. There were three adults and a small child. The woman was the first to talk.

"Hi, there... Oh, Honey, don't look so stressed. You're in good hands here. I'm Auntie, this is my husband Uncle, and my brother, Bear. That little man over there is Johnny. You've been sleeping for days and haven't woken once. The bathroom is right there if you need it. Go ahead and do your business and I'll explain everything after." she said, with concern in her eyes.

I rushed to the toilet and emptied my bladder, washed my face, and gargled with the mouthwash sitting on the counter next to the sink. I lingered, trying to delay facing the four strangers in the other room, but eventually I got the nerve to join them again.

Auntie had made up a plate of food for me. I sat at the place set for me, but I wasn't hungry. I drank and emptied the glass of water.

"If you want more water, help yourself," she said, pointing at the tap.

I got up and drank three full glasses, taking the fourth back to my seat.

"Where is Moose?" I asked, barely able to hold back the hysterical sobbing that came next. I sat bawling my eyes out. No one said anything. I sat head down with my hands wringing in my lap. My long greasy hair covered my face. I was afraid, filled with self-pity, and ashamed of myself. I was very confused about what had happened. Where was I? How did I get there? The two men got up and left, taking the baby with them, leaving Auntie to calm me down.

"Aw, listen Honey, don't worry Moose will be back. I'm his aunt. You don't have to be afraid. You're safe here." I felt better, and slowed my hysterics a pace or two, but didn't say anything and didn't stop crying.

"Eat something. You haven't eaten in days, it looks like." she urged.

I wiped my running nose on my sleeve and pulled myself together as best I could. I tried to eat some of the cooling food in front of me, but after only a couple of bites I felt nauseous and full at the same time. I pushed the plate away and asked if it was ok to just go lay down again. She laughed and waved me off.

"Can you at least tell me where I am?" I asked, before I left.

"Don't worry. You're still in Verdun. Just a couple of blocks over from Prickles and Granny. I think that's where Moose is now. Bear probably went to find out. Don't worry, girl, you're alright."

I went back to the room and fell back into bed. I buried my face in the pillow, and started to cry again. I must have fallen asleep, because when I awoke, Moose's booming laughter had joined the mixture of voices outside my bedroom door.

Moose didn't have any profound explanations about what had happened to me for the last couple days, just that I must have overdosed. He said I was totally out of it, but still got up and walked around with prompting and help. Prickles had kicked me out, he said. Moose led me around until he could find somewhere for me. Auntie and Uncle agreed to let me stay in exchange for childcare during the day, but Moose continued to stay at Prickles.

I saw less and less of him over the next couple of days. I started to feel better. Auntie and

171

Uncle were good people. They fed me, paid me a pittance, and kept me clean and sober. Johnny was a great kid, too, and we spent most of our days together watching TV and colouring pictures.

Moose got more and more into drugs and crime. In those last weeks he even met with my father to try and extort money from him. Moose threatened to turn me out as a prostitute if he didn't pay. My father made some threats of his own, but never gave in to the shakedown.

One afternoon Moose showed up just as Auntie was getting home from work. He wanted me to get ready because we were going to see his parents.

I was surprised. He had never mentioned his family before, and Auntie told him she didn't think it was a good idea. He just ignored her warnings and hurried me to get ready.

It was early evening when we set out. We took the metro, then got on a bus, then another bus, and then walked for what felt like hours. I was completely lost, and whining about being cold and tired. He just walked head down lost in his thoughts, like a man on a mission. Finally we came to the house. It was a large cottage-style home, set back with a long driveway leading up to it.

We knocked on the door, and Moose's younger brother answered it. They embraced tensely, and little brother said almost in a whisper, "Mom will be happy to see you, but he's here, too, you know."

"Who is it?" Boomed a woman's voice from the other room.

"It's me, Mom. Smells good in here. What's for dinner?" Moose said.

We rounded the corner into the dining room, and there sat his mother and Him. Mom jumped up and came to hug Moose and shake my hand, but Him just sat there.

Mom rushed into the kitchen to fix us a plate of lasagna, or maybe just to get away from Him and Moose.

"I told you not to come here anymore. What the fuck do you want this time?" Him said, in a deep near-whisper. I wished I could melt into a puddle on the dining room floor.

"I needed to talk to you." Moose said

"You don't know how to use a fucking phone?"

"I wanted to talk to you face to face." Moose offered.

"So, talk."

"Well I was hoping we could do it in private." Moose said, nodding in the direction the hallway.

Slave to the Farm

"You bring this lovely lady all the way from wherever the fuck you came from, and now you want her to sit here alone, and wait for you. Always the gentleman, eh Moose? She looks like she froze her ass off getting here. Sit down, Sweetheart, Mom will fix you up," Him said, pushing back from the table and heading towards the hallway ahead of Moose.

Mom came back and offered me some food and a warm cup of hot chocolate. I smiled thanks, and started nibbling on the lasagna. Little brother had disappeared to his room, and Mom and I sat there not speaking. She just watched me, and I felt very uncomfortable and naked under her gaze. I tried not to show it.

"You and Moose going out?" she asked finally. I nodded, but didn't say anything.

"Well he's my son and I love him, but if you want my advice, get as far away from him as possible. You look like a nice girl. Go home to your parents. Moose has a lot of problems."

As if on cue, the voices from the other room grew louder as an argument heated up.

"You don't marry a man like Moose...you belong to him. Big difference you know. He's not a lot different from Him in there," she said, lighting up a cigarette.

I looked up at her, and felt sorry for the woman. Suddenly, she looked hollow and defeated. I gave up on my dinner, and stared into the cup of hot chocolate. We sat in silence, listening to the murmur from the other room.

Finally, Moose come back into the dining room, but didn't sit down.

"Come on, we're out of here," he said, handing me a black leather jacket. He went around and hugged and kissed his mother, while I stood up from the table. Little brother came around the corner to give Moose another squeeze before we headed back out the door.

"So, what was that all about?" I asked, on the long walk back to the bus stop. Moose didn't answer. I was thankful for the jacket, as the night had grown colder. We tread along the rural road until reaching a small depanneur. In the parking lot, we saw a car idling away while the owner was inside the store. Moose tried the driver's door. It opened, and he jumped in, leaning across to open the passenger side door for me.

"Get in."

We drove the car to Verdun and abandoned it four blocks from Auntie and Uncle's apartment. Moose walked me to Auntie's door and then turned and left without saying anymore.

Slave to the Farm

Confused, but very happy to be back, I gave up trying to figure out what the whole thing meant, and seriously considered taking Moose's mother's advice. I didn't want to let Auntie down after all she was doing for me, but... the fates played their hand first anyway.

Within a day or two of the visit, Moose and Prickles were arrested. Someone came to Auntie and Uncle's to tell us the news. Immediately, I walked over to see Granny, because I thought that Prickles wouldn't be there. I was wrong.

The apartment was on the third floor of one of Verdun's many row houses. I climbed the stairs and let myself in. I looked into the living room, but no one was there. I walked down the hall to the kitchen at the back, where Granny's bedroom door was located but as I rounded the corner, I saw Prickles and Granny sitting at the kitchen table. The saw-off 410 was also sitting on the table in front of them.

Granny saw me first, and I knew in an instant from the look on her face that I had made a mistake in coming. Prickles swung around and caught sight of me too. He grabbed the gun and pointed it right at me.

"You fucking rat. You did this." He screamed at me.

There were more people in the kitchen than I had first noticed, and Picasso was one of them.

"Come on, man. Put that fucking thing down" he said, but Prickles swung his loaded eyes towards him, and told him to shut up. Picasso just stood, not saying anything in reply.

Prickles, still pointing the weapon at me, asked, "So what do you have to say for yourself, you fucking narc?"

"I don't know what you're talking about. I didn't rat on anyone. I just wanted to know what's going on," I blasted back, surprised that I wasn't more afraid.

In fact, at that moment, I wanted nothing more than for him to shoot me. I was tired of being on the run and feeling like I didn't understand what was happening all around me. I was tired of not having any choices, and I was already convinced that my future was hopeless. Death seemed like the most pleasant option.

"Go ahead and pull the trigger, asshole. You'd be doing me a favour." I baited him.

Everyone in the kitchen erupted at the same time, trying to calm the situation down. Prickles just sat calm with me firmly in his sights, and I glared back, surprised at my own calm.

Finally, he stood up and laid the gun on the table before charging me. He grabbed me and

dragged me down the hall to the front door.
Opening it, he heaved me down the first flight of
stairs. I was up and running before he could get a
hold of me again.   Prickles never came past the
first flight. I stood out on the street collecting
myself, while he screamed down the stairway. He
said he would kill me if I ever came back.

I wondered what I should do next. I had to
go back and get my things from Auntie's. It was the
only thing I could decide on. I came through the
alley, and in through the back door. I heard voices in
the living room, and headed towards them to see
who was there.

It was the police talking with Uncle. Auntie
came up behind me with a bag of my stuff from the
bedroom. It was pretty obvious they were there to
arrest me. I was relieved in a way, and went with
the officers willingly.

A night in the stainless room at L'Escale,
then the grey van to collect me in the morning, I
was actually glad to see the Farm when it came into
to view. The strip search, the lice shampoo, and the
three-day room program, it all seemed like a
welcomed routine that I was too long getting back
to. I was on my way back to Baillie, but even that
was OK. The only dark cloud I could not shake was
thinking about facing Beasley. She had been telling

me over and over how proud of me she was. I'd let her down again by running.

Slave to the Farm

Slave to the Farm

James Taylor

Beasley came to Bailie to see me as soon as she could. I was in the bath when she got there, and she knocked and came in, relieving the staff supervising me. She looked me over. Her eyes said it all. They were filled with concern, pity, and disappointment.

"My god Erika, you have lost so much weight. Have you eaten anything over the last couple of weeks? I see you got some more tattoos too. Why? You were so beautiful. Why, Erika? Why did you run? You were doing so well, and now I don't know if you'll be able to come back to Renaissance."

Her words cut me to the bone. I felt ugly, unlovable and undeserving of forgiveness. Her expression verified that. I sat mute, filling the bath tub with my tears.

181

Slave to the Farm

"Well, don't worry. I'll do all I can to get you back to Renaissance. The choir really misses you. I'll need your help though. You do want to come back, don't you?" She asked, brushing my wet hair away from my face to see my eyes. I nodded, but continued to say nothing.

"Missy was especially worried about you. She said she saw you last weekend in Verdun metro and that you looked very... unwell. She didn't want to tell on you, but she was scared. She could see how much weight you had lost and said you looked dirty and out of it. She found out where you were living from some other people she knows in Verdun."

I was surprised that Missy narced on us. I felt betrayed and relieved at the same time. I remembered seeing her in the metro one day, but had thought she hadn't seen me. I never thought twice about it.

The cops had first gone to Prickles apartment to look for me, but found Moose instead. That is why Prickles hadn't been arrested. The cops hadn't come to arrest anyone for crimes, they were there looking for run-aways. I guess after Moose had been arrested, he told them where they could find me a couple of blocks over. I'm pretty sure it wasn't out of concern for my well-being, but for a promise of leniency.

Moose was back on The Farm, too, but was placed in the highest security cottage, Chapel. We would continue to write each other for a couple of weeks, but I never saw him face to face again on The Farm.

Beasley relentlessly advocated for my return to Renaissance. Every day she was on shift, she came to see me in Bailie and brought her reading list with her. She had me write poems, and letters to Head-Honcho begging him to OK the transfer back to the lower security cottage. My parents started coming every Sunday again, but their disappointment was weighty, and our visits very strained. They weren't so sure the move to the open cottage was a good idea.

After a number of weeks in Bailie, however, the move was approved. Again I made the short trip across campus to Renaissance.

I fell back into the routine of the cottage and returned to school. I rejoined the choir, and was relieved to be back in Renaissance, with all the girls making me feel welcome again. I even forgave and thanked Missy for turning me in.

Lizard was happy to have me back as a singing partner, and we resumed our never-ending Rummy game.

There were weekly group meetings in the cottage. We sat together in the common room, and aired grievances or dealt with day-to-day issues that came up in the house.

It was also the time to make requests. I certainly wasn't in a position to make many requests, but I did make one. "Could I have a roommate?" I had been alone in Bailie without a roommate, and even though I had been back a couple of weeks in Renaissance, I was still in the intake room alone. I wanted to bunk with Lizard, of course, but I was denied. The staff told me I was manipulative. They didn't want me influencing the other girls. I didn't quite understand what they meant. It was nice to have someone to talk to at night; I didn't want to manipulate anyone. In the end, I did get a new roommate when a new girl needed the intake room for orientation.

I finally got a letter from Chapel. I was surprised when it wasn't from Moose. It was from another guy named Stretch. I had no idea what prompted the unsolicited letter, but I did remember him from Springfield cottage, before he did whatever it was that put him in Chapel. We had never really spoken that I could remember. He told me he was a friend of Moose's, and that Moose was on a room program (solitary confinement), so wouldn't be able to write or get letters from me for at least a month, maybe longer.

What he didn't tell me was that the room program was for fighting, or that Moose had been fighting with him. I never really got the complete story, only parts of it from here and there, but I continued to receive mail from Stretch every day or two. I didn't always write back, though. I was suspicious of him. I asked the girls in the cottage if they knew him, and the consensus was that he was a nice guy. I started writing him back every now and again. True to Stretch's first letter, a note from Moose never came for me, and my letters to him remained unanswered.

After a couple of weeks, Stretch wrote to say he was being moved back to Springfield within a couple of days. He asked if, when he got his privileges, 'would I walk with him around the circle?' I told him to talk to me when he got out.

A couple of days later, I saw him smoking on the steps of Springfield in his housecoat. It was the open boys unit right next door to Renaissance. He didn't yet have the privilege of his clothes, or the right to go back to school.

One Monday morning, as I left the cottage to walk to the school building, Stretch caught up and walked with me.
He was very tall, and had mulatto skin with green eyes. We walked together to and from school all that week. But because he had no privileges, that was all the socializing we could fit in.

We went to the gym to play floor hockey with Springfield cottage one evening, and Stretch and I played on the same team. We continued to get in trouble for not paying attention and talking too much.

We lost every game we played. Eventually, Stretch and I could walk miles together around the circle, and our participation in sports improved.

After about a month and a half, I got an angry letter from Moose. He had been sprung from his room program and was granted letter privileges again. He called me all sorts of demeaning names and told me I was a nigger-lover. I wrote back telling him he had it all wrong, but he wouldn't hear it. He just kept writing me nasty letters.

Eventually, they got threatening and I considered letting Beasley read them. I told him that's what I would do if he didn't stop. Fearing another room program, his letter-writing campaign stopped.

My relationship with Stretch grew. As the school year wound down, a dance was planned for those who were graduating. I wasn't one of them. I had missed so much school that year that they considered failing me yet another grade. There was only one girl from Bailie and three guys from L'Avinir graduating that year. Every open cottage was invited to the dance anyway though, and I went as Stretch's date.

We primped and preened and wore our best clothes. We did our hair and nails and looked forward to the party with heightened enthusiasm. It reminded me of the night long ago when many of the same girls did the same thing in Le Village, readying themselves for a visit from Springfield.

Finally, the girls of Renaissance were ready for their night out at the gym. I wore a beautiful turquoise dress and white high-heeled shoes. My hair was feathered and I had a ton of makeup on my face.

Slave to the Farm

The gym had been decorated and the lights dimmed with a disco ball splattering lights off the walls. There was fruit punch and finger foods on a buffet, and loud music playing out the speakers. Everyone had a great time dancing and talking and hanging out, but mostly we enjoyed the slow dances.

I danced with many people that evening, but all the slow dances were with Stretch. There were quite a few staff milling around with cameras. My picture was taken numerous times with different people, but one of Stretch and I became the trigger that motivated Moose to start threatening me again, and the catalyst to another room program for him.

Moose wasn't at the dance, of course. No one from Chapel was, but somehow a picture of Stretch and I made it into the locked unit. Moose immediately wrote me a threatening letter, saying I was making him look like an idiot. I was a slut. He was gonna kill the fucking nigger who stole his girlfriend. I wrote back that he was an idiot and a bigot. I told him I wasn't his girlfriend and never would be again. I reminded him if he wrote me again, I would show the letters to staff. Apparently, he flew into a rage and found himself locked in his room, or so the rumor mill went.

I got one more letter from Moose with nothing but a picture of Stretch and me together. It said 'I love you' on the back. I showed it to Stretch but he said he had never seen it before. I didn't believe him, he must have been the one to set the whole thing up, but he just denied, denied, denied. I finally let it drop and kept the picture.

alice cooper

Beasley and I continued talking and getting closer. I learned to trust her more and more, and began to tell her personal things about myself. My privileges were being reinstated one by one and finally I reached the level where weekend visits were a possibility.

Beasley worked hard at getting me a weekend with my family, but continued to face resistance from Head Honcho. I was just too much of an AWOL risk.

She told me 'they" believed I was holding back and not really getting to the bottom of my emotional troubles. Beasley said she believed I was working really hard but wanted me to dig deeper and find out why I kept running away.

I tried to explain that I didn't really know why. I just ran. I wanted to live on my own. I was fifteen years old and had been in and out of placements for a couple years already. I didn't think my family wanted or loved me. If they would just let me out, I said, I could get a job and an apartment.

Slave to the Farm

She wasn't at all convinced. I suggested that I could get welfare and try going back to school. I wanted to work with animals, and particularly horses. I said I would gladly shovel shit, but no program could be found that would give me experience or offer me a job with horses. Nothing ever presented itself.

"Erika, you don't want to be on welfare or shovel shit for the rest of your life. You're too smart for that. You deserve more for yourself."

I wanted to believe her, but I didn't think I was too good for anything. I believed that if I had my own place I could make a go of it.

However, that's not the way the system works. Once you are made a ward of the court under the Youth Protection Act, what you want for yourself is rarely considered "in the best interest of the child". If some organization claiming to be acting on your behalf finds it beneficial, then maybe you've got a chance. Beasley and I kept digging.

One Thursday afternoon the cottage was quiet. Beasley and I were the only ones there. Everyone else had gone to the gym with Beaton to play volleyball. I was too excited about my first weekend home in months starting just fourteen hours later to think about sports. I sat drinking instant decaf coffee and talking with her in the office. We'd made the rounds of our usual topics: school, choir, family, friends, and boys.

Suddenly Beasley asked me if any boys had

ever been sexually inappropriate with me. I went cold. I couldn't think of a single time she had asked me a direct question about being sexual abused.

She had given me many books on the subject, and I always knew they were to encourage me to talk to her about it, but I never brought it up.

I thought long and hard about what secrets I should share. I'd never told anyone about being raped, and losing my virginity to a beast. I'd come close to talking about it with her before, but something always stopped me.

I sat struggling, trying to decide what time to tell her about, or even if I should tell her anything at all. She watched me mulling the question over, and I could read the anticipation in her face. Her eyes screamed... Do it! Say it!

"I was raped the first time I ever had sex." I blurted out.

Her face relaxed and I could read multiple messages in her eyes simultaneously: sympathy, relief, concern, curiosity. I just sat staring at her, regretting having said anything. I didn't want to continue with the questions I knew were coming next.

"Who did it to you? When?"

I was quiet for a long time, weighing out my options. I didn't want to tell her the details, because I didn't want her to tell my parents. I certainly never wanted to talk to them about it.

"If I tell you, you'll tell my parents." I countered.

Slave to the Farm

"Well no, not necessarily. We don't have to tell them right away, but I think they should know about something like this. Don't you?"

"NO!"

"Ok, ok, don't worry; I'm not going to say anything. Why don't you just trust me and we'll work it out together?"

"I don't want the cops involved, either." I sniped. "I don't trust those assholes."

"No cops. No problem." she assured me.

I suddenly had this desire to tell her everything. I just didn't want to carry the weight all by myself anymore. I had been stumbling into trouble before that fateful night, I had run away, dyed my hair black, and even been arrested. The problems had already started. I was already smoking, drinking, and had tried a number of drugs. As much as I wanted to believe it was the reasons for all my emotional problems, I knew it wasn't.

"It was a couple weeks before my fourteenth birthday." I started and told her the story I hadn't told anyone before.

"I was with my father in the United States. We were going to a wedding. The bride was my father's cousin. Most of the night I sat with him, my grandmother, and a bunch of other old people I didn't know. I was totally bored. The bride's daughter was about eighteen or nineteen years old, and was sitting at a table near the dance floor with a bunch of her friends. She kept looking at me till finally, she came over to ask if I wanted to join them. I gladly accepted and started drinking with them right away. They had pitchers of rye and ginger ale at the table, and all I needed was a glass. I got a buzz on, and started dancing with all the young people. We danced and laughed for hours, and one by one groups of people started leaving. I was sitting at the table taking a break when Jon, one of the guys with our group, pulled up a chair next to mine. I was sitting parallel to the table and so did he facing me with our knees almost touching. He asked me if I wanted to come to an after party with them. I told him I didn't think my father would let me. It was almost midnight already. He put his hands on my thighs and rubbed them up under my skirt. I sat frozen for a second, not knowing what to do, but then pushed my chair back and stood up. He acted like nothing happened. I just walked away and headed towards my father's table.

I met Dad halfway across the dance floor with my cousin in tow. She excitedly told me, before my dad could say anything that he had said I could come with her for the night. I looked at my dad to confirm it, and he nodded his consent. We left shortly after, piled into a little car and drove over to a house party. There were many more people there than had been at the wedding. We stayed drinking until very late. Five of us left together: my cousin, Jon, and myself in the back seat with another couple in the front driving.

My cousin was very drunk. She kept passing out in the back seat and by the time we got to Jon's

Slave to the Farm

house she was really out of it. Jon and I helped her
into the house, and laid her on the sofa with a
blanket.

Jon said he would show me where I could
sleep. He brought me into a bedroom with a bunk
bed in it, and offered me a t-shirt to sleep in. I took
the shirt and waited for him to leave, but he didn't.
He just stood there watching me.

I didn't move. He moved over behind me and
reached to unzip my dress. I froze. He unzipped
while I clutched the dress up to my chest. He came
around the front of me and waited for me to drop
the dress. When I didn't he ripped the dress from
my grip. It dropped to the floor and I stood there in
my underwear with my arms still covering my
breasts. I couldn't look up at him in the face. He
pushed me back onto the bed and covered me with
his body. He started feeling me everywhere and
trying to kiss my mouth. I resisted, turning and
twisting my head away from him, pushing his hands
away from my body. Suddenly, he slapped me in
the face and I cried out and started to cry.

"If you wake someone up, I'll kill you!" he
whispered in my ear.

I lowered my voice to a whimper. He grabbed
my panties and ripped them from my body. He
forcefully spread my legs and tried to force his way
inside me. My whimpering and crying grew louder,
so he slapped me hard across the face again to quiet
me. I left myself. Suddenly all I could see was his
back.

The next coherent thought I had was of being alone. The sheets under me and my thighs were bloodied. I just balled up in a fetal position and tried to be as quiet as possible.

I must have finally falling asleep, but was awoken by a telephone ringing in the other room. I heard a woman's voice answer it, and seconds later she knocked and opened the bedroom door. She told me my father was on the phone and wanted to know if I was ready to go home. I just nodded. She said she would wake Jon to take me to my aunt's house.

"NO!" I heard the fear in my own voice.

She looked questioningly at me. I asked her please to tell my dad to pick me up. She obviously knew that something was wrong, but didn't ask what. She agreed and left the room.

I got up and dressed. I looked at the bed. It was stained with my virginal blood. I thought of ripping the sheets off the bed, but suddenly Jon was there in the doorway. He followed my gaze to the bed, but said nothing. The woman came in behind him to give me the message that my father was on his way. Her eyes too fell on the rumpled sheets, and the expression on her face changed. She looked from Jon to me and back again, but said nothing. She spun on her heels and left us. Jon stood for a moment longer before he turned to me and mumbled under his breath, "If you say anything to anyone, I'll tell them you begged me to do it slut."

I just stood there feeling like a very little girl. I didn't understand what I did wrong. I didn't understand why he hated me so much. I was terrified of him. I couldn't look at him. I just stood staring at my feet. He left closing the door behind him.

I had to pee so badly but was afraid to leave the room, so I got on the bed and pissed into the bloody sheets. My parts were stinging and I felt like his penis was still inside me. Finally, my cousin knocked on the door and opened it.

"Your dad is outside," she told me, and without a word I pushed past her and ran through the living room out to my father's car."

As I was finishing my story, the other girls started trickling in from the gym. I sat there drained, feeling like I had just moved a whole mountain stone by stone. I was tired. It was the first time I had told anyone about that night, but I didn't really feel relieved. In fact, I wished I could take it all back. Beasley got up from her chair to hug me, but I shrugged her off and ran to my room. I hit play on my tape deck, and listened to the Lynard Skynard cassette I had cued in the player. *"Simple Man"* blasted out the speakers and I sang along crying out my excess emotion. The music made me feel better: normal. By the time dinner rolled around, I was back to my moody teenage self. It was a few hours closer to my weekend and that was all I could think about.

I just let the confession I'd made to Beasley slip away into oblivion.

Slave to the Farm

Morning dawned and I woke with a hop in my step and excitement bubbling in my stomach. One more day of school and I'd be on the bus home for the weekend. I got ready and headed down to the kitchen to get some breakfast. There was staff everywhere, including Head Honcho. I was surprised to see them all. What were they all doing there?

Not having much time before first bell at school, I just ate with the other girls and left for my day. I was surprised at lunch when they were still there, sequestered in the office discussing something serious.

We ate lunch, guessing at what the big meeting was about. No one really knew, but we all agreed it probably wasn't good. The afternoon classes crept by, but finally the last bell rang. I hurried back to Renaissance to pack my weekend bag down to the front door to load into the van when it got there.

While I was in my room, Beasley knocked and came in.

"Erika, I need to speak with you." she said, but I could see she was struggling with something. Dread settled in my heart.

"We've been in meetings all day, as you know, and we want to speak with you."

I thought for a millisecond that maybe it was good news but after studying Beasley, I realized that it wasn't good. I got panicky inside, trying desperately to figure out what I had done. I didn't have any idea, but was sure I was about to get busted for something. I followed her down the stairs and into the office where Head Honcho and Duck Walk waited. Head Honcho was the first to speak.

"Now, Erika. We need you to understand that it is our responsibility to keep you safe while you are in our care. We take that responsibility very seriously. We can't very well send you into an atmosphere that is unsafe, and for that reason we have decided to delay your weekend pass until we can get more information," he said making my head explode into an instant migraine. I burst into tears.

"What are you taking about? What unsafe atmosphere? I've done all the things I needed to. I promise I will stay at my mom's all weekend. I won't AWOL. I promise. Beasley what are they talking about?" I sobbed, looking pleadingly at her to speak for me. My head was reeling trying to think of where all of this was coming from. The confession the day before never even entered my mind.

"After what you told Beasley yesterday, we can't in good conscience let you go home to your parents where it might be unsafe." Head Honcho continued.

"What the fuck are you talking about? My parents have always protected me. They have never abused me, why would they this weekend? What I told Beasley yesterday doesn't have anything to do with my parents!" I screamed out, staring at Beasley with daggers in my eyes.

She had betrayed me, and I wanted to pull all the hair off her head. I wanted to scratch out her eyes, and stomp on her dead body. She was wringing her hands and wouldn't look at me. I couldn't read the expression on her face, but it looked a bit like regret. The next sledgehammer blow to my soul nearly made me wretch right there on the floor.

"Now, Erika," Head Honcho continued, "yesterday you told Beasley that your father sexually abused you..."

"That's not fucking true! I never said that! I NEVER SAID THAT!" I wailed at the top of my lungs. "You're a fucking liar! Why are you doing this to me? I fucking trusted you! I fucking hate you!! I told you everything! Why are you doing this to me?"

No one said anything at first. I sat sobbing with my face buried deep in my hands. I felt like I was in a bad dream, and I couldn't wake up. I thought of my parents and what they would think. I already felt a million miles from my mom and dad. This would make the divide even wider. I continuously felt like a burden, an impediment, and a handicap to bear. They were so unhappy, and I knew I was a big part of why. I was such a disappointment to everyone. I was sure my mom hated me. This would just be the icing on the cake.

I wanted to die. My head was hammering away, and I thought I was going to throw up.

"Erika, I don't know what to say, but maybe if

199

you read what I wrote in your log yesterday we can talk about it." Beasley offered softly.

"What the fuck for. You just made it up anyway. I don't want to talk to you ever again."

The meeting was over. I shut right down. I didn't answer any more questions, or even look at anyone. I sat like a stone, not hearing, not thinking, just dying inside. I could feel the acids in my stomach burning into my throat. I didn't even hear them when they dismissed me to my room. Head Honcho had to wave his hand in front of my face before I acknowledged he had spoken to me. Like a zombie, I stood and walked out.

I stayed in my room not eating for two days. Staff came and went to check on me, but I was always in the same position. I didn't speak to anyone, or answer if they asked me a question. I even sent away the girls that came to bring food. They tried to make me feel better, but I didn't want anyone's sympathy.

Sunday morning crested, and visiting day was upon me. My parents never missed a Sunday. A knock came at my door, and one of the girls told me they just saw my parents' car at the gate. My head started throbbing, my blood pressure rose, and I felt hot and bloated, but I didn't get up. I knew Beasley would come any second to try and coax me down for my visit, but I set my resolve against it.

When the knock came, I rolled over and looked at her for the first time since the meeting. She seemed pleased but hesitant.

"Your parents are here for your visit." she said cheerfully.

"Tell them to go home, or better yet tell them anything you want, I don't care. You're all liars anyway. I'm not going down there." I hissed at her.

"Erika, they drove all the way here. The least you can do is go and see them yourself. Don't you think?"

"No, I don't think. No one asks me what I think or what I want. No one cares, and they are all liars anyway. Go tell them I don't want to see them" I said with finality, and rolled over turning my back to her. She stood for a moment longer then went down to tell them I wouldn't be visiting with them that Sunday.

I spent one more night in my toxic self-pity, but rose the following morning and got ready for school with a new resolve. I would just do my time, and get out of this fucking prison. I knew they couldn't keep me forever.

There was a sigh of relief from all the girls in the kitchen when I rounded the corner, and plugged in the kettle. Now things could get back to normal in the cottage, they thought, but everyone continued to walk around on eggshells.

By Wednesday I was feeling better, but it wouldn't last long. At lunch while I was walking back to the cottage, I noticed Head Honcho's car parked outside the unit. My stomach clenched up and I knew that he was there to discuss my confession. I slowed my pace and delayed getting to the front steps for as long as I could, but eventually I just put my head down and pushed ahead.

The office door was closed and the lunch routine was well underway. No one came to collect me for the slaughter, so I sat and ate with the other girls. We did our after meal charges, and went to the common room to have a smoke before going back to school.

Just as we were getting ready to leave, Duck Walk came in, and told me stick around.

"Can you just hang out here till we're ready for you, please?" He said.

All the girls cast their sympathetic eyes towards me as they filed past, hurriedly trying to get out of the building as quickly as possible. I lit another cigarette and tried to calm the storm brewing in my bowels.

"We're ready for you now, Erika," Head Honcho called from the office. "Can you please come join us?"

I sat defiantly finishing my cigarette before I got up, and like a dead man walking headed towards the office.

I came face to face with my parents, Duck Walk, Beasley, and Head Honcho. I felt like a burnt offering smoldering on an altar. I sat in the chair set out for me facing all the adults, feeling more and more like a target.

Head Honcho, the mouth piece, of course started the conversation, "First, I want to thank all of you for coming. I know this isn't easy for any of us. Erika, I would also like to say that I'm glad to see you're feeling better." I gave him the finger.

"Anyways, as I was saying.... blah, blah, blah." I quit listening and didn't really hear what he said. They all just talked among themselves, while my thoughts flew away into the mists. I didn't look at anyone and didn't offer anything to the conversation, but suddenly I realized they were all looking at me expectantly waiting for an answer.

"I don't know." I offered.

"Were you even listening?" Head Honcho asked.

"You don't listen to me. You don't care what I think. No one asked ME if I wanted to be here. What do you want from me? I don't care anymore."

"Well Erika, if you had been listening, you would have heard me say that we are thinking of letting you go home this weekend. In fact, if you want, you can pack and go home for a long weekend right now."

"Oh and what about being in danger?" I snipped.

"Well, as you have retracted your statement and you father has led us to believe that perhaps a grave misunderstanding has occurred, we are willing to give you the benefit of the doubt." HH said shuffling the papers in front of him.

"I didn't *retract* my statement. She lied. I never said what she said I said." I spat out, pointing an accusing finger at Beasley who cast her eyes to the wall.

I looked up at my dad.

"Dad, I never said it. I swear." he looked away, unable to hold the sight of me in his hurt disappointed eyes. I couldn't tell if he believed me or not. I hadn't given him too many reasons to trust me lately. I felt ashamed and contrite. Even if my parents believed I didn't say it, they knew my dirty little secret. How could they love me now?

"Well, either way," Head Honcho said, "Do you want to go home with your parents now, and come back in the van Sunday night?" He asked again.

I sat and thought it over. I wanted very much to get out of the cottage, but the thought of riding the hour and a half to Beaconsfield in the back seat of my parents' car wasn't very tempting. I came up with a compromise. "What if I stay till Friday and ride the bus back to Montreal with everyone else?"

Everyone's head swung in my parents' direction. We waited to see what they had to say. My mom started crying but nodded her head.

My dad said, "If that's what Erika is comfortable doing, that's fine with us."

"Good, it's settled then. Erika, you'll go home on the bus this weekend, and just keep working with Beasley in the meantime. Thank you again for coming. Erika, you can go back to school now. We'll let them know to expect you."

I got up to leave and my mother rose too. She came to me, and wrapped her arms around me, but I stood like a statue.

"I love you." She said through her tears. Over her shoulder, I looked at my dad. He wore a defeated sad expression. He looked tired. Finally he looked up at me and gave me a feeble 'thumbs up.'

I left and went back to school, relieved it was over.

Many years later, I talked to my dad about that time. We'd become much better friends over time, and I felt more comfortable asking questions I'd held inside for years. I brought it up to him because I wanted to know more about the wedding where I was raped. Were there any pictures? I wanted to try and identify the man that raped me. I knew his first name, but I wanted more. I knew my dad's cousin should know who had come with her daughter that night, and whose house my dad picked me up at. I wondered if she had a picture of her daughter's date. I really wanted to see a picture of Jon. All I could really remember of his looks was his dark curly hair, his thick eyebrows and how he looked from the back.

Dad told me he would do what he could. He went on to tell me sketchy details of something that had also happened twenty-five years earlier.

While all this was going on in 1985, my father lived in a small bachelor apartment. One morning, someone from Shawbridge called him to a meeting downtown Montreal. He said he thought it was a lawyer but wasn't sure. He wasn't even sure exactly where the meeting took place. Anyway, this guy accused him of molesting me. Dad said the guy was really aggressive, telling him he had evidence, and that he was going to put him in jail. He threatened to charge my father with incest, and told him that if he confessed, it would be better for all involved.

My father vehemently denied the accusation, and left the meeting in search of his own lawyer. He doesn't remember ever going through with hiring one. He said that was the only time he was contacted about any sexual abuse. He didn't have any memory of the meeting I described above at Shawbridge, and doesn't even remember any Shawbridge staff actually mentioning anything about me being raped to him.

The whole event is a bit of an enigma. It wasn't until I sent my dad on the search for Jon's last name and picture that my family began talking about what happened to me at that family wedding. It seems that after I admitted being raped by Jon, Shawbridge went on an incestuous fishing expedition. When my abuse turned out not to be my father's doing, they dropped the subject entirely.

After the weekend visit at my mom's, Shawbridge never encouraged me to report the actual rape, and very little if anything was ever mentioned about what I said really happened to me.

Twenty-six years after that wedding in Pulaski, New York, I learned Jon's full name and studied pictures of him. I wrote a letter to the New York State Police and reported the incident even though the statute of limitation had long passed. Justice isn't what I hoped to achieve. I don't believe any justice system has the power to deliver a piece of someone's soul back. But finding missing information can. Information can free a person's soul. I was convinced by my younger brother that maybe I had information that could help some other woman. Maybe I had a piece of information someone else was looking for. Grandiose thinking? Maybe, but worth the price of a stamp.

The Pulaski New York State Police never sent me a reply.

Slave to the Farm

Slave to the Farm

Twisted Daisies

From the shadows, lurking, his eyes did creep. Upon daisies so
fresh and so sweet.
With all the trust in one grain of sand, he plucked up those
daisies to crush in his hand.
What man, what demon, what boy is this, to take what is
straight and make it twist?
What woman, what maiden, what child is me, to hide and to
secret what happens to we?

Our sons and our daughters, our mothers and fathers, when
shall we rise above,
 Do what is needed, for the daisies just seeded, and finally learn
how to love?
Our brothers, our sisters, our daisy fresh whores; they hold the
secrets to losing war,
It's silence that blinds us and makes us not see, the cycle of
violence heaped upon we.

Slave to the Farm

With raven's vision and help from the crow, we'll keep
planting daisies, row upon row.
Setting flowers blooming all over the earth, who have control
of their bodies and when they give birth. And lurking in
corners, the wolves who are sheep, will wither and slither and
die in their sleep, and we will no longer wonder how this came
to be, this sexual slavery forced upon we.

So twisting in silence, daisies still grow, hiding the secrets that
all flowers know,
Like, we are the ones we've been waiting for; whether seeds of
a daisy or GMO whore.
And we tend to our garden with shovel and hoe, using the shit
that all daisies know,
staking the flowers all broken and hurt, silently twisting till
they compost to dirt.

ROXANNE

Rox- anne - You don't have to put on the red light

THE POLICE

I told myself I wouldn't run after all the excitement of my rape confession, but after just a few weeks, I couldn't take the stagnant air on The Farm anymore. I didn't really have any concrete plans. I just wanted a couple of days to myself. I knew when they finally caught me, I would wind up in Bailie again, but I didn't care. The unpredictable hours between this moment and that one were all worth it.

So one morning in the spring of 1985, the grey van drove me to St Mary's hospital in Cote-des-Neiges for a medical appointment. I AWOL'd from the hospital minutes after they dropped me off. I just walked right out the front doors and got on a bus. I got off near Atwater and wandered around inside the Alexis Nihon shopping centre, then headed up St. Catherine's towards downtown. I people-watched, and window-shopped along the way, but didn't really have a destination. I decided I might hang out in the plaza outside Place des Arts. That was as far as any of my plans went.

211

Slave to the Farm

I was getting hungry. I walked right past Place des Arts and down to St. Laurence and Ste. Catherine Street. There was a Burger King on the corner where I planned to get a hamburger. I squeezed past the four prostitutes huddled in a scrum blocking the door way.

As I was standing in line, I noticed a couple more prostitutes coming out of the women's washroom. I didn't really look at them, just shifted out of their way as they walked past. One of them stopped in mid-stride.

"Erika, is that you?" She asked.

I focused my attention on her. At first I didn't recognize her. It was Lollipop. She was very much dressed for the part she was playing. She had knee-high patent leather boots on, a mini-skirt, and skimpy bra under a bright fuchsia satiny jacket.

I thought, she must be freezing in that outfit. The thick makeup she wore made her look much older, and very different than when I last saw her in Le Village. We embraced, and she asked what I was doing there. I told her I had AWOL'd and was hanging out, looking for something to do. She invited me to her apartment, but said she wasn't finished 'working'. She told me she only had to do a few more tricks, and we could get out of there.

It was about 5 P.M. and I told her I would eat my hamburger while I waited. She headed out with the other girls to join the huddle outside

I just sat eating, looking up every once in a while to check if Lollipop was still there. One time she wasn't. I wondered if she would be gone long. Minutes later, there she was, standing all alone.

I went out to talk with her. We chatted while she kept a close eye on the street, calling out to the cars that crawled by. One stopped, and she bounced over to the passenger side window to talk to a older man in a nondescript car. I couldn't hear what they were saying, but I assumed that she would get in the car with him. She didn't. She came back to stand next to me.

"No deal?" I joked, as she took up her position again.

She turned to me very seriously and said, "He wasn't interested in me. He was asking about you. I told him you weren't working today."

I hadn't considered that the Johns driving by would be looking at me as a possible prostitute. I was wearing a pair of old jeans, a t-shirt and a jean jacket with no make-up. For some reason, I thought that no one would look to me for sex, because I was obviously not done up like the other girls.

Apparently, none of that really matters to men looking to pay for sex. As long as we have all the proper parts, we are all potential whores. The idea that he had thought of me as a hooker made me very uncomfortable in my skin. I wasn't judging Lollipop for being in the sex trade. 'Live and let live', as they say. But I was grossed out by the fact that a man older than my own father was trying to buy me.

A second vehicle pulled up alongside the curb.

"You girls want to have some fun?" the passenger called, from the window of a white van.

Lollipop approached the van and looked in the window towards the back of the truck. She turned to me and said, "There are only the two guys in here. You want to come?"

They were young guys, maybe in their mid-twenties, but that didn't motivate me to want to join her. I shook my head and she started negotiating with them to take her alone, assuring them she could handle them both. A deal was struck, and she hopped into the van with the two guys.

"You sure you don't want to change your mind. We are nice guys, you know. We'll pay you guys extra to come together." the passenger pleaded once more, but I shook my head, and said I'd wait there. I went back into the restaurant to smoke the cigarettes Lollipop had given me.

After three or four smokes, I really started to worry, because she wasn't back yet. I wished I had memorized the plate number, but had never thought of it till then. There was a new group of girls standing outside, but I didn't recognize any of them from before. I didn't know quite what to do next. As I built up the nerve to go out, and talk to the girls outside, I spotted Lollipop walking up St. Laurent towards the Burger King. I felt a flood of relief swell in me, till I noticed that she didn't have her jacket with her anymore. I rushed out to meet her and see if she was alright.

She was alive, that much I was thankful for, but it was obvious that it had been a bad date. Her face was puffy where she had been struck and her neck looked purple with finger prints left behind after someone had tried to choke her. Her jacket was missing, so she lumbered along half naked in the cool spring evening.

When I got to her, I noticed a welt on her back like she had been whipped with something. She starts apologizing as soon as she spied me.

"Erika, I'm so sorry. You must have been worried. I'm sorry I took so long."

"Are you alright? What happened?"

"I'm alright; I'm alright... its ok. Jerks got my jacket though. Fuck them anyway, I boosted a wallet." she cackled, as she produced a leather wallet from somewhere in her mini-skirt. She peeled it open, grabbing the wad of money and threw the rest of it in the doorway of a closed building for someone else to find.

She counted $375 in the wad, liberated some bills from it, and gave me a $100 to stick in my pocket and stuck the rest into the back of her skirt.

"You wait here. I have to go see someone and I'll be right back," she told me as she headed up Ste. Catherine Street. I just hung around in the doorway looking down at the discarded wallet, not paying attention to what building she had gone into.

Slave to the Farm

I smoked the last cigarette, and watched the cars drive by. Some would slow down, eyeing me lustily, but when I didn't come out to the curb to speak to them, they drove off.

I couldn't wait to get out of there. Night had descended. Everything looked grungier and more ominous. Finally, I saw her coming out of Les Foufounes Electriques. I walk over to meet her and together we headed to St. Laurent metro station.

We took the metro to Charlevoix to score some weed in Pointe St. Charles, then got back on the metro heading towards Berri. At Berri, we transferred over to the orange line heading north towards Henri-Bourassa.

At Jean Talon, a woman and three small children got on and sat directly across from us. At first, I didn't notice anything, but Lollipop began squirming in the seat next to me. I could tell something was wrong. I looked up at the family across from us. The woman stared intently at Lollipop. The young children, the oldest not more than 6 years old, sat quietly, oblivious to any drama. No one said anything. We just stared at her and she at Lollipop. The Metro slowed as it came into Jarry station, and when it came to a complete stop, the woman herded the three children off the train. The doors closed before Lollipop said anything to me.

"That was my mother and my two little brothers and sister. I haven't seen them in at least two years. What a trip. Ravi was just a little baby last time I saw him."

"Why didn't you talk to them?" I asked.

"My father has forbidden my mother to speak to me. I've disgraced the family, he says. He won't talk to me, either. The only one in my family I've seen or spoken with in years is my older brother. He came to tell me I was disowned, and not to call the house anymore."

I didn't know what to say. We just sat in silence, both thinking our private thoughts. I didn't understand why her mother hadn't said anything. How would her father even find out she had seen Lollipop? I wanted to ask her why she wasn't in the system anymore, but guessed if her parents quit calling the cops when she went missing, the cops quit looking for her.

I couldn't see my family disowning me for anything, and felt sorry for her.

"Well, fuck it anyway. I'm happier now. My father used to beat me all the time. I'm better off without them. I just wish I could talk to my brothers and sister sometimes," she said, looking deep into her wringing hands.

"Yeah, I miss my brother, too, sometimes."

We relaxed in her barren two-bedroom apartment, smoked weed, and ordered some take-out. Her roommate wasn't home, which made Lollipop happy, because she was pretty sure Mr. Mr., their pimp, would want some money for letting me stay there. She said what he didn't know wouldn't hurt *her*, but that her Roomie told him everything. I asked Lollipop why she even had a Mr. Mr. Couldn't she just do the same thing for herself?

She turned sullen and quiet. I regretted saying anything.

"I'm sorry. It's none of my business," I said, under my breath.

"He pays for this apartment. He buys me designer clothes, and paid to have my broken tooth fixed. He protects me and buys me things. I've known him since I was nine years old. I trust him. You don't know him, but he's a good man. He takes care of me."

Again, I told her it was none of my business, and regretted making her feel defensive. We lit a couple cigarettes and sat in silence. The spell was broken by a knock at the door. The food arriving was a welcome diversion. We were both starving, and as we sat eating our fried subs, we moved on to lighter happier topics.

The next morning when I woke up, I was alone in the apartment. We had shared her single bed, and I was surprised I hadn't woken up when she left. I wondered what time it was. I checked the rest of the apartment, and confirmed that no one was there with me. I checked the cupboards and found everything I needed to make coffee.

I was just finishing my second cup when Lollipop walked in the door, but she wasn't alone. Somewhere she had met up with Roomie. They sniped and bickered at each other about this and that, but I was sure the problem really was me being there. The conversation eventually came around to my presence.

"Well, you know Mr. Mr. doesn't want us having people over here, especially if they're not working," Roomie said, with obvious disdain for me.

"It was only for one night and you weren't even here. If I had kicked her out first thing this morning, you wouldn't have even known. Come on, give me a break. It wasn't like I was having sex for free... like you like to do," Lollipop tossed back. "I don't tell on you, but I could."

"Okay, okay, you keep throwing that in my face. I won't say anything, but she can't stay here tonight." Roomie pressed. "Get her out of here today!"

"No problem. We'll go somewhere else tonight. Okay?"

"Okay." Roomie said, slamming the door on her way out.

We left the apartment sometime late in the afternoon and headed back downtown. Lollipop left me in a greasy little cafe while she went to meet up with Mr. Mr. I waited and waited and waited some more. I even thought that she might have abandoned me there on purpose, but I still had most of the hundred she had given me yesterday, so I could leave anytime.

Finally, she came back.

"Sorry for making you wait so long. I'm glad you didn't leave. Roomie, that bitch, ratted me out. She told Mr. Mr. about you."

"Was he pissed?" I asked.

"Well, kind of, but he said he already knew. He saw us together last night. Said he figured we would head back to the apartment eventually. It's no big deal really, but he wants you to work. That's what took so long. I got him to let me do your tricks for you tonight. He said you can live with me while I show you the ropes. We can start tomorrow night. What do you say?"

"Lollipop, I don't want to do tricks," I said, getting up. "Maybe I should just leave right now."

"Hang on, don't go yet. You don't have to do anything tonight. I did it for you."

"That's not what I mean. I don't want to do it tomorrow, either. I just wanted to hang out with you, that's all. I can't do what you do." I said with a little more arrogance than I meant too.

"You mean you're not a whore like I am, right?" she spat back.

"No, that's not what I mean, either. Look, I'm sorry, I didn't mean to piss you off, I just think sex is fucking gross. Whether you get paid or just do it for fun. Guys are such pigs, like those guys yesterday. I don't want to do it as a job."

"I don't like doing it, either, but I make a lot of money. Those guys yesterday just didn't want to pay. I could have left without the money, but they deserved to get robbed. I do it because it's easy and men are stupid. They will pay you for anything, like this one guy who pays me $500 every couple of weeks to stand naked while he throws oranges at me. Oranges!! I don't even have to touch him. He jerks himself off. I don't like doing it, because he's a weirdo, but it's an easy $500, and he doesn't touch me. I just go somewhere else in my head, like I imagine I'm skating. I skate, I skate, I skate, then it's over. It gets easier after a while."

I didn't answer. I sat staring at the table. I didn't think it would ever get easier.

"Not all the Johns are bad you know. I even like a couple of them," she went on, but again, I didn't answer.

"Anyway, we don't need to think about it till tomorrow night. Tonight we are gonna listen to some reggae, smoke some weed, and eat some awesome Jamaican food. Let's get out of here," she said, pushing away from the table and looking expectantly at me.

I slowly got up and followed her out of the cafe.

We took the metro to Namur, and then walked over to Mountain Sights just as it was getting dark. We knocked at an apartment door and a very small boy answered. Lollipop said hello and asked if Tosh was home. The kid just opened the door wide without answering. There were three adults and four children in the apartment. Lollipop introduced me to the group, who all stared at me like I was an alien. I felt very uncomfortable under their gaze. I was the only white person there and had never found myself in the position of being the cultural minority before. I felt the racial undercurrents acutely. It seemed like an eternity before someone said anything.   Finally, the only woman, an older heavy set Jamaican woman offered to make us something to eat and the atmosphere lightened.

Marley busied herself in the kitchen, and the smells made my mouth water. She served us Curry chicken with rice and peas. There was a side plate of plantain too. It smelled delicious, but my limited palette struggled with the unfamiliar spices. My hunger, on the other hand, won out over any pickiness and I ate heartily.

Afterwards, we listened to music and smoked weed as people came and went from the apartment buying baggies of pot from Tosh. The four boys eventually went to bed, and we sat playing round after round of Rummy.

It started getting late, and I wanted to leave. I hadn't said more than twenty words all night, most of them please and thank yous, so I just tried to send Lollipop telepathic messages, not wanting to bring any attention to myself. Finally, she said, "We better go."

We took the metro back to Henri-Bourassa. Roomie was there when we got back to Lollipop's place.

"I told Mr. Mr. about her, you know. He wasn't very happy. He's gonna be even more pissed at you tomorrow," she said, not even looking away from her TV program.

"Go fuck yourself," was all Lollipop had to say to her, as she slammed the door to her bedroom behind her. I lay down in her bed and fell asleep almost immediately.

The next morning we rose to an empty apartment. We lounged around most of the day, finally leaving the apartment sometime after 4 p.m. We headed downtown and made a couple stops along the way to eat and smoke with friends of Lollipop's.

Eventually, around 6:30 p.m. as the sun was setting, we got to Lollipop's work corner. There were a couple of other girls there already working. They were somewhat hostile towards me.

"Who the fuck is this newbie?" one of the girls asked Lollipop, while the other scanned me up and down.

Lollipop and I hadn't really talked about what was expected of me, and I felt panic well up inside of me. I didn't know how to get out of the situation I was only beginning to realize I was in. I had just avoided thinking about it all day. I was expected to turn tricks for my room and board, and standing there at that moment, I didn't think I could do it. I was terrified at the prospect of trying.

Slave to the Farm

"Ginger, give her a fucking break. She's here cause Mr. Mr. wants her here. If you got a problem with that, go see him."

A car pulled up to the curb before anyone else could say anything. The girl who hadn't said anything approached the passenger side window and started negotiations. She turned to look at the group of three of us standing under the covered awning of a closed shoe store. Cantankerously, she said, "He wants the white chick."

My heart leaped into my throat. The last thing I wanted to do was go anywhere with that man. I felt like crying, but I held my poker face, or what I thought passed for disinterest. Lollipop saved me once more by telling him we weren't working yet, to choose one of the other girls.

"Fucking whores; get in!" he said to the girl at his passenger door window. She did, and they drove off. My head was reeling. My heart rate started climbing, and I heard my pulse pounding in my ears. Ginger sucked her teeth at us, and stomped off to find another corner or talk to Mr. Mr. I would never find out which. Lollipop could see my discomfort and anxiety, and tried to make me feel better.

"Don't worry about her. She's always a bitch to the new girls. She's just mad you're prettier than her. It's not as bad as you think it is. You'll make money and it will get easier, trust me. The girls will love you too. It just takes time for them to get to know you. You only got to do two tricks tonight and you can work more when you don't feel so scared. I'll be here to help you." she said, reaching out to hug me, but I didn't feel much better.

Another car pulled up to the curb. Lollipop approached the passenger door. I couldn't hear what they were saying, but Lollipop turned to me and said she'd be right back. She climbed in the car, and it pulled away leaving me alone. I still had about $60 from the money she had given me days before, and I thought about taking off to the metro, but instead, kind of stood in a daze. My stupor was broken when another car stopped at the curb and called out to me.

He was a young East Indian guy, maybe in his mid-twenties. He looked clean-cut and was very soft spoken. "Get in" was all he said, and like a zombie I open the door and climbed in. I didn't say anything and neither did he. He pulled back into the street and slowly drove up St. Laurent, and just kept looking over at me. Eventually, he reached down and undid his pants, exposing his penis. He reached for my hand, and I just went along with whatever he wanted. I gave him a hand job, and when he was finished and I was sitting there with his spunk in my hand, I realized I hadn't asked for payment first.

He pulled over to the curb many blocks from where he had picked me up.

"Get out." he told me with a growl in his voice.

"You didn't pay me," I said, rather more meekly than I intended.

Slave to the Farm

"And I'm not going to, whore. That's why you get paid first, you dumb bitch."

I reached for the door handle wanting to get out of the car as fast as I could. Right before I closed the door I flung his cum back at him. I saw him wiping it from his chin as he drove away, taking that very small victory with me I headed back towards Lollipops corner.

My first trick and I didn't even get paid. I was too embarrassed to go back and tell Lollipop what happened. I decided I would make for the closest metro and head for the West Island but before I could find one, a police cruiser stopped me. An officer got out to question me.

"Are you out working tonight?" the cop asked in French.

"Non."

"Do you have ID?" Again in French I answered no.

"What's your name?" he asked, but I didn't answer.

The cop started asking me more and more questions, some of which I didn't understand with my limited French. I just stayed silent. Finally, I told him I didn't understand French. He laughed, and in broken English he told me he was arresting me. For a fleeting second I thought of running, but ended up just getting in the back of the cruiser when he opened the door. The Farm at that moment seemed like safe haven. He took me to the police station.

226

Slave to the Farm

I was left alone in a room with nothing but an empty desk. A cop eventually came in and asked what my name was. I told her it was Christina Davis. I had fake ID under that name that said I was twenty years old, but not with me. I'd been arrested and released under that name before but without the cards I had my doubts. I was hoping that maybe they would release me again. I told her all the information I had memorized from that identification and she left to verify my lies.

Minutes later I was taken to lock-up. I was locked into a single cell, facing a much larger one, where a number of men were locked in together. There was a toilet in my cell, and even though my bladder was about to burst, I couldn't bring myself to use it in front of all the men in the other cell. Mother Nature, however, won as she always does, and while I relieved myself amid the cat calls of a man watching, I wondered if the insult of this day would ever end, but the day wasn't over yet.

After everything calmed down and the prisoners relaxed back into the boredom of captivity, a young policeman came to the front of my cell. He looked in at me and unlocked the door.

I got up off the cot I was sitting on, because there was something about him that unnerved me. His movements and carriage gave me chills. He stood shadowing the doorway, not saying anything, just looking at me like I was a prized pig up for bid at an auction.

Slave to the Farm

In French he told me to put my hands up against the wall and spread my legs. I did as I was told, and assumed the position.

He moved farther into the cell and stood behind me. He leaned in and took a deep sniff of my hair. Goose flesh rose all over my body.

He bent down and rubbed his hands up one of my legs, cupping my vagina before rubbing them down my other leg.

A drunk man in the cell across from me screamed out something lewd, and the cop told him to shut up. He turned his attention back to me standing with my hands pressed against the cinder block wall. He put both his hands on my shoulders and rubbed them down my back. He grabbed my ass as he put his hands deep into my jean pockets. Next he put his hands on my hips, hooking his thumbs in the waist of my jeans. His hands met as they rounded my body stopping on my stomach. I was wearing only a t-shirt, no bra. They had taken the bolero jacket Lollipop had lent me earlier.

The cop ran his hands up my body, cupping both my breasts, and kneaded them. I pushed hard against the wall and spun around spitting at him. I hastily backed away from him, and dropped into a fetal position in the corner. The men watching in rapt attention from the other cell burst into a loud uproar, whistling and cat calling and making a ruckus.

The cop started towards me huddled in the corner, but stopped in his tracks when the door into the cells opened. Three more police came rushing in to see what the commotion was about, but only found Lover Boy leaving and locking my cell behind him. The three said nothing to him, but started yelling at the men in the communal cell to shut up and settle down. All the cops went away together, leaving us prisoners to our own personal hells.

I stayed with my knees hugged to my chest on the floor next to my cot. The men in the cell across from me could only see my toes sticking out past the bed. One man kept calling to me, asking if I was OK. He said he had seen everything, if I needed a witness. He kept screaming obscenities at the absent cops.

I never answered or looked at him, just sat silently weeping. Before too long, the door into the cell area opened again and two plain clothes policemen came to stand at my cell door. The female cop called to me by my proper name.

"Are you Erika Tafel?"

When I nodded yes, they unlocked the cell door and asked me to follow them. I was left in the same room I had first been in with the desk, but now I knew I was waiting for the grey van to L'Escale. I was offered something to eat and drink, but declined. I said nothing about what happened in the cells.

I was surprised the next day when I left L'Escale, and was brought to Le Village instead of Bailie. I was dropped off and processed into Le

Slave to the Farm

Village to start my three day room program, almost
relieved I was there. My social worker from Ville
Marie came eventually to see me. He told me that
there were no beds in Bailie, and that was why I had
to stay temporarily in Le Village. I liked Le Village
better than Bailie anyway, and fell into the routine
of Village life easily. Beasley never came to see me
there though.

In the following weeks while at Village, my
father rented a two bedroom apartment in
Beaconsfield. It was just a couple of blocks from
my mother's house. He started talking about me
moving in with him.

I think my father started wondering if maybe
the system wasn't as good for me as my parents had
first thought. My venomous mouth and perpetually
angry attitude became more and more pronounced
while placed in the system. The constant reminders
that this was all for my own good wasn't working.
Scaring me straight wasn't working.

I was no longer the sad confused little girl I
used to be. Now, my depression took on more adult
dimensions. I talked about wanting to die. How I
didn't want to grow old. My disdain and mistrust of
authority figures was obvious and often bled over
into my views of all adults.

My father's attitude change made us stronger
allies. I didn't know at the time that he had been
threatened by one of Ville Marie Social Services'
lawyers, or that they were harassing him for money,
but I noticed the change in him.

Slave to the Farm

The parents of kids on The Farm were charged a sliding scale fee based on family income. They wanted the maximum payment from my father, based on our combined family income. He refused to pay. That may be why, when I finally made it back to Renaissance and reunited with Beasley, we went to work right away on getting me released into my father's custody. It took a couple of months. I spent the holidays on The Farm, and sometime in early spring I was released to live with my father.

Slave to the Farm

Slave to the Farm

I Shot The Sheriff

I shot the sheriff, But I didn't shot no de-pu-ty Eh—No— No—

Bob Marley

It went pretty well at first. I liked the apartment and it was close to all my friends. My dad was easy to live with, and not really demanding. He didn't require me to let him know where I was every second of the day like my mother did. As long as I came home at a reasonable time, we rarely argued. It ran relatively smoothly for months until I had a party in the apartment while he wasn't home one night.

One of my 'boyfriends', snooping around the apartment, found and stole my dad's 303 rifle. I didn't know at first, but my dad soon noticed it missing. He confronted me about it. I heard about the theft from other friends, so I wasn't surprised when he brought it up, but hoped he just wouldn't notice.

We started fighting and arguing when I wouldn't tell him who took it. Some stupid code I was living by: I didn't want to be a rat. I know he wanted to call the cops and report it, but we both knew that would lead me right back to Shawbridge, this time with charges. The cops were never called.

Our relationship started deteriorating quickly. He had no reason to trust me...again. I started spending more and more of my time away from the apartment, trying to come home when he wasn't there or was asleep. He would never wake me in the morning, and I don't even know if he ever checked to see if I was there. I didn't go see my mother or brothers, even though they had come faithfully every Sunday while I was locked up. Finally, when I did see my dad, he told me that my mother was very concerned, and thought that I should go back to Shawbridge.

I started to panic. I begged him to let me stay, making all kinds of promises I never meant to keep. He told me to just go to bed, and we would talk about it in the morning with my mother. Then he took my apartment keys away.

As soon as I heard the inevitable rhythmic snoring gathering momentum from his bedroom, I collected some things and left. I didn't even risk trying to get my keys from his night stand, instead I left my window slightly open so I could get in if I had to.

Slave to the Farm

I got the hell out of Dodge, so to speak, but after a couple of days on the run, I needed to get back into my father's apartment where my meager belongings were. So, in the middle of a work day, I scaled the brick wall to our second floor balcony and crawled in through the window. I ate something, careful to make sure it wouldn't be obvious I was there. I took a shower and was just searching the apartment for my set of keys when I heard someone at the door.

"Shit! Someone must have seen me breaking in."

I went to the door thinking it would be a neighbour or the superintendent and quickly opened it up.

All the wind in the apartment was sucked out into the hall when I came face to face with my mother. At first I couldn't breathe, she certainly didn't except to find me there, and at first she didn't recognize me. I just stepped back from the door and let her in, closing the door behind her.

"Where the hell have you been?" she started. "We've been worried sick."

She told me there was a family meeting with my social worker, and I had to come. They were deciding whether or not to put me back on The Farm. I told her I wouldn't go back, no matter what. We argued and she backed up blocking the door so I couldn't leave.

In all the years of bickering and screaming and harsh words between my mother and I, we had never physically fought. That day we did. It was the first and last time.

I grabbed her and shoved her hard to the ground before getting myself out the door. I cursed her for blocking the door like that. Why did she make me hurt her like that? I tried to erase the sound of her crying as I left, but my mind just kept replaying it. Why didn't she just let me go when I asked her to move?

She had interrupted my departure, so now I had even fewer belongs. I had nowhere to go, because I didn't have any time to make phone calls, so I walked around the streets of Beaconsfield wondering what my next move was. About an hour later, a police car came around a corner and upon seeing me turned on their flashing lights.

I had a split second to decide to run or not, but I decided to try the fake name routine.

It worked to a point. I had the cop convinced I wasn't who he was looking for, but told him my ID was at home. I was just walking over to a friend's house. He insisted I get in the car and he would drive me to my house for the ID, and then drop me off anywhere I wanted to go after he confirmed I was who I said I was.

I was trapped, and as I climbed into the back of the cruiser I came up with a plan. I gave him my neighbour and best friend Juju's address because I knew I could just walk in. He drove off toward her house.

Slave to the Farm

My plan was to get out of the car and head straight for the backyard of Juju's house, assuming the cop would follow me. I would go in through the back door and straight out the front before he could catch up. He was in his sixties and overweight, so I thought all I needed was a small head start. I was betting he wouldn't chase me on foot too far.

It didn't quite work out.

The first glitch was Juju's brother, Monkey Man, and all his punk rocker friends hanging out in the driveway when we pulled in. The cop got out, opened the back door for me, and I stepped out looking Money Man right in the eye. I willed him not to say my name out loud. Without saying anything to anyone, I headed right for the back-yard. It was my second mistake. The cop didn't follow me. There was no easy way out of the back-yard except through the house and out the front door. It was fenced in on all sides.

I went into the house through the back door and could hear the punkers arguing at the front with the cop. They were trying to keep him from entering the house. I thought about finding somewhere to hide in the back yard, but Juju found me hesitating in the back laundry room. She rushed me through the house and pulled me upstairs. Even before I reached the top, I realized my third mistake. There is no way out from the top floor.

The cop finally made it in the front door, and saw me at the top of the stairs. He started up the steps immediately, and I started right back down them. I placed my hands on the wall and the banister to lift myself, and planted a two-footed kick square into his chest. He crumbled from the impact, and ripped the banister from the wall as he tumbled backwards down the stairs.

Everyone was in shock as I jumped over the prostrate cop in a heap at the bottom of the stairs, and ran out the front door, only to find my mother standing in the driveway, wondering what all the commotion was about.

I ran past her at first, intending to just keep running. But she called out to me, and for some unknown reason, the tone in her voice made me stop and give up.

Before the cop even had time to get out of the house, I turned around and got into the back seat of the cruiser. The cop recovered from his spill, got into the car behind the wheel, and drove me to the police station in Kirkland, snarling at me in the rearview mirror.

I was isolated in a room while the appropriate people were contacted, and I started the wait for the grey van that would bring me to L'Escale for the evening, or so I thought.

Before any of that happened, though, a man in a suit with yellow paper came into the room to question me about what happened in Juju's house. I described to him my version of events, including the two-footed kick. He asked me a few more questions and left, never really telling me what I was being questioned for.

Eventually, the van picked me up, but instead of dropping me off at L'Escale, they drove me straight to Bailie's door, and I started my reintegration into Farm life after almost six months of being away.

I soon found out the cop I kicked was considering charging me with assault. That was what the questioning was all about at the station, I was told.

I got lucky, though: the charge was dropped when the prosecutor decided the judge would have a tough time seeing my hundred pound frame assaulting a two hundred and fifty pound veteran police officer.

The police even paid for Auntie Elvis' banister repair.

Slave to the Farm

BACK DOOR MAN

The men don't know — but the lit He girls un-der-stand —

THE DOORS

I started school again and tried to stay out of trouble, but it didn't last long. I went AWOL and was arrest again right before Christmas in 1985. I spent the holidays in Bailie that year. I got two beautiful L'Espirit designer sweaters from my new primary. I was impressed by the sweaters, but not really by her.

I thought of her as a drill sergeant. Rigid, hard and cold. I don't think she liked me very much, either. I counted down the days till I went back to Renaissance.

By early 1986, I'd made it back to the open cottage. I was sixteen. I slowly gained back my levels and was doing well, but in the waning winter months I got another chance to run.

A school friend, CareBear, introduced me to Brutus and Vega. They both worked for a local West Island snow plowing company. She liked to ride around with Vega while he plowed, and I began going with Brutus on his route.

Vega and Brutus lived together, so after long hours of snow clearing the four of us would head back to Ste. Genevieve and pass out. I stayed at Brutus and Vega's apartment most of that winter.

I think because Brutus and I spent so many long hours together in the truck, it kind of just morphed into a physical relationship at home.

Not a healthy one, however. I certainly don't remember falling for him in any way. He was grumpy, moody, and mean-spirited. I think when he started being nice to me, I was so relieved I fell for it. As soon as we started sleeping together the violence began.

It was nasty little insults at first, then hair pulling, pinches and charlie-horses, but it started to get more and more physical almost on a weekly basis. I started hiding bruises. I often knew from the first look on his face in the morning if I was going to get it that day or not.

Vega tried not to notice. He started keeping Brutus and I apart as much as he could. He'd invite me to come with him whenever he had somewhere to go, and I always agreed even if it meant sitting in the truck for hours.

As fate would have it, early one morning someone recognized me at a local fast food restaurant while I was out snow plowing with Brutus, and called my mother. She called the police and I was arrested and returned to the Farm.

Slave to the Farm

In June of 1986, I went to court in Kirkland and was sentenced to another six months in placement.

By the end of that month, I left the Farm for the last time and moved into St. James group home in NDG. I didn't even last a week before I went AWOL for the very last time ever.

I went back to live with Brutus and Vega. I no longer had a sexual relationship with Brutus, but for some reason we continued to fight like we did. He got violently jealous if I paid attention to any other guys... except Vega?

Vega helped find me a full-time job in a small sandwich shop and drove me to and from work as often as not. He taught me to drive his car on l'Ile Bizard and we spent more and more time together.

Despite our best efforts to avoid it, Vega and I started having an affair. It didn't last very long. I was deathly afraid Brutus would find out and kill both of us, but the awkwardness of the whole situation forced Vega from his own apartment, leaving it for Brutus and I.

I felt abandoned and scared, but I refused to turn myself in this time, or get caught at any cost. I stayed in the empty abusive relationship thinking I had nowhere else to go.After Vega moved out, I took the bus to work.

One afternoon, while waiting at a bus stop, Super-Mac recognized me and offered me a ride home.

Slave to the Farm

He was a friend of Brutus'. We'd met for the first time the previous winter while I was riding along with Brutus on his snow-removal route. Super-Mac was plowing driveways of his own at the time. I thought he was cute, but hadn't really thought of him or seen him again till that day at the bus stop.

Super-Mac started coming over pretty regularly after driving me home that day. I would get all giddy inside when I saw him at the door. He and Brutus would talk cars and the renovation business they both worked in. They would drink a case of beer and then, predictably, Super-Mac would suggest going somewhere. Brutus never wanted to go anywhere, so Super-Mac would turn to me and of course I always did. We would take off on Super-Mac's motorcycle. Brutus never seemed to notice our attraction to each other, or if he did, he didn't seem to care.

August 13, 1986 was Super-Mac's twenty-first birthday. He called to invite me out for a celebration drink. We planned to go to The Marina on Lakeshore drive and I was so excited because Brutus was also leaving for the weekend that same evening. He didn't have to know anything about the Marina and I didn't tell him.

I couldn't wait for him to leave. I just tried to act nonchalant, but I was just itching to get rid of him so I could start getting dolled-up.

The minutes tick-tocked agonizingly away till he finally lumbered out with his weekend bag. I

244

was never alone with Brutus again, except for the one time he nearly killed me.

Super-Mac and I spent the weekend together in the apartment and on Sunday night when Brutus was expected back I thought Super-Mac would just leave before he got there, but he didn't.

Brutus came crashing through the door and seemed a little surprised to see Super-Mac there. My heart was racing but nothing happened. The three of us just sat awkwardly watching T.V. until I got up to go to bed.

Again, I thought Super-Mac would say his good-byes and go home, but instead he also said goodnight and followed me to my bedroom.

Brutus said and did nothing. I was terrified all night but nothing happened.

Every day after that weekend Super-Mac would drop me off at work, and pick me back up again. We spent all our free time together. Brutus never said anything to Super-Mac or me about our obvious relationship.

Super-Mac never left me alone with Brutus though, not even for a second. This went on for about two weeks.

One afternoon, on one of my days off, I was alone in the apartment while Super-Mac and Brutus were out working. It started raining.

Every drop filled me with more and more dread. Sometimes Brutus would be sent home if the weather was too bad to work outside. I decided, to be on the safe side, I should get out of the apartment as quickly as possible.

I jumped in the shower, but before I was finished, Brutus smashed open the bathroom door and pulled back the shower curtain. He stood staring at me in the shower.

I tried to grab the towel hanging on the rack next to the shower, but before I could get it wrapped around me, he grabbed me out of the stall. We started fighting. He just kept calling me filthy names. I was trying with all my might to get away from him, but I was losing the battle.

He had a death grip on one of my wrists. He kept wrenching me around by my arm, body-slamming me into walls and dragging me over chairs.

In a last ditch effort to free myself, I grabbed a handful of balls. Wrong. His eyes exploded into fiery embers of rage. He grabbed me with both hands around the neck and forced me up against the wall. He lifted me off the ground, and was choking off my air. My toes stretched as far as they could, searching futilely for the ground. I clawed at the noose of fingers around my neck, knowing I was going to die.

After the first moments of sheer terror passed, there was almost a calm; the inky black corners in my vision started pooling deeper and deeper. But I didn't die. He let go.

I slid down the wall gasping for breath, my legs unable to hold me up, my own hands now wrapped protectively around my own neck. I was dizzy and disorientated. I was weak and my vision unsteady.

Super-Mac rushed over to the heap that was me collapsed in the hallway, while Brutus escaped out the back door.

It took me a second to realize Super-Mac was there. I was afraid I would be choked again. I tried to get away from him thinking he was Brutus. I stopped struggling when I realized who was holding me. Eventually, I let him embrace me while I sobbed in his arms.

We sat on the floor holding each other until I calmed down. He looked into my face, and then at the finger impressions on my neck, and shook his head in disgust.

I started pulling myself together, and realized I was naked. I suddenly felt ashamed of my bruised and battered body. I pushed him away trying to cover myself from his view. He got up and found the blanket from the couch to wrap around me.

"When you're ready, pack your things. We're moving. Tonight!" he said, then went to make some phone calls.

Within a week, Super-Mac and I had our own apartment. I still had the waitressing job Vega had found for me, and after a few months, Super-Mac encouraged me to petition the courts for my freedom. We lived together, off and on, for the next nine years.

Slave to the Farm

Warrants for my arrest were still circulating. I contacted my Ville Marie social worker to see what could be done about them. I told him I had an apartment, a job, a stable partner, and I wanted everything dropped. I told him I was happy, healthy, and that if I got arrested I would only run again, and again.

He said he would look into it, and by the turn of 1987 all warrants were dropped. I was free, and no longer a ward of the Quebec juvenile system. My indentured servitude on 'The Farm' was over. I was seventeen.

I got used to not looking over my shoulder all the time. My relationship with my family improved, my parents got back together, and Super-Mac and I started spending holidays with them. I was finally growing up, and started building a life of my own.

River City Junction

The Farm theme has never left my life. After the Shawbridge Boys Farm chewed up and spit out my teenage years, I found it strangely comforting that the man I would eventually marry, have children with, and build my life around, spent his whole life on "The Farm" too. A different farm, thousands of miles from where I grew up. But he lived on The Farm nonetheless.

His farm had cows, pigs, and chickens. My Farm had animals of a different sort. His had locked gates, holding pens, and line-ups for medication. So did mine. And sometimes he felt as trapped on his farm as I did a slave to mine.

He lived on the Farm when I met him, and I even lived there with him. However, I felt miserable and despondent there for too many reasons to talk about here, so I hatched my new plan to escape from that Farm too.

Slave to the Farm

But I just couldn't do it. I found I'd lost my nerve for running. I just couldn't leave like a thief in the night anymore.

With a little maturity, I was forced to think this AWOL through. I had children of my own now to think of. I had to decide whether to take them with me or leave them on The Farm with their dad.

Even more paradoxical, I wanted their dad to run away with me. I loved him. I didn't want to leave him at all. I just couldn't live there any more.

For him it was home. For me it was like constantly walking on eggshells again.

He was the only son and had many responsibilities on that family Farm. Responsibilities that had been his since he was a little boy. His work, his income, his family, and everything he had ever known was right there for him. Would he leave that all behind to jump into the void with me?

He was much more courageous than I gave him credit for at that time. He did jump into the void with me, and I didn't even have to beg. I laugh when he tells people how I saved him from 'The Farm'.

Our land called to us from our sleep. We left his family farm and bought a farm of our own.

My husband had many childhood dreams of the house he would one day build. I just had dreams of the front door. A strong solid door to lock myself behind, but only if I wanted or needed to. That door

Slave to the Farm

symbolized security to me. It meant I could be safe, warm, and most important... home.

We called to the land, and it called to us. I've never felt as safe as I do here. Now we homestead off-grid in the shadow of Anarchist Mountain in the Boundary region of British Columbia.

We built the house we live in, and are in the process of building another. We have chickens, and pigs, and dogs, and cats, and horses, and more.

I can't help feeling I've come full circle, arriving right back at the proverbial Farm gate.

My definition of The Farm has changed over the years, and has been the difference between life and death for me in a hundred different ways. It keeps redefining itself as my life marches on.

The Farm is still as much a part of me now as it was in the 80s.

It somehow became part of my cellular make up. Somewhere, for some reason, I was handed a life sentence: Life On The Farm With No Chance Of Parole, and really... there is no place I'd rather be and no role I'd rather play than being a slave to my farm.

Slave to the Farm

*Glossary:

Academic avoidance: Skipping classes.

Acid: Lysergic acid diethylamide is a hallucinogenic drug. Also known as LSD, sid, blotter, or micro-dot.

Altar of Ass: A toilet.

Amcal: A placement for juveniles in Kirkland Quebec.

AWOL: Absent without leave

Bad trip: A very scary reaction to any drug ingested.

BHS: Beaconsfield High School

Bling: Slang for money or something of worth.

Catholic education: Public school boards in Quebec are divided between Roman Catholic and Protestant, with estimates of up to 30% of Quebec high school students attending private institutions.

Communal underwear: Every morning we lined up to choose a pair of socks, a bra, and underwear, along with our clothes for the day. To get the privilege of my favorite pair, I had to race to be first in line. I hated it when I didn't get my favorite panties.

Compulsory school system: Prussia claims the first modern compulsory system that was recognized worldwide and copied. They introduced this model with a goal of more obedient soldiers and serfs. Laws based on this model reached the united States in 1850s, and Canada soon after. Inspectors and politicians were among the first to argue for school compulsion and drafted the laws needed. The orphaned children of many of the immigrants to the New World were homeless and living off petty crimes. The new compulsory schooling laws and newly introduced child labour laws made rounding up these impoverished children possible. Housing became a problem, with many children being sent to adult prisons. Reformatories and residential schools were built to fix this problem (see Shawbridge Boys Farm). Education is compulsory between ages 6 to 16 in the province of Quebec.

Depenneur: A convenience store.

Education: I added this because I wanted to point out that true education to me is the natural process of information assimilation from personal experience. Schooling, which is often confused with education, I believe, is a political tool used to manipulate, condition, and limit the natural process of information assimilation from personal experience.

Excited States: The United States of America.

Ex-Lax: Name brand laxative that is flavored and looks like chocolate.

Gold stamp: The name of some hash circulating in the 1980s.

Greenhorn: Inexperienced.

Green Death: A name used to describe Export 'A' brand cigarettes that come in green packaging.

Hash: Cannabis plant resin pressed into blocks that ranges in color from light brown to almost black. Also known as hashish or black hash. See Gold Stamp.

Hazing: A humiliating and sometimes dangerous initiation ritual.

Herpes-zoster: Medical name for shingles. From the same virus that causes Chicken Pox.

Homeschooling: As the name suggests, homeschooling means schooling at home, however there are many different ways to achieve this education. Some other names for this are unschooling, deschooling, and self-learning.

Joint: The name of a marijuana cigarette. See spliff.

Jungle juice: A concoction of alcohols usually stolen from a parent's liquor cabinet and mixed together.

Juvenile diversion program: A neighbourhood program that aims to give teens activities and a place to meet.

Juvenile system: The federal government enacted the *Juvenile Delinquents Act* in 1908 with a stated goal of making the treatment of accused delinquents more of a social welfare exercise than a judicial process. The *Juvenile Delinquents Act* was philosophically touted as the state intervening as a "kindly parent" in situations where a family could not provide for the needs of its children. See Youth Protection Act.

Juvy: Slang use to describe the juvenile system and the kids in it, e.g. "She is a juvy on the run." or "They'll put you in juvy, man, if they find ya."

K-Way pants: A name for a brand of water proof garments that was popular in the early 80s.

Lachine Shelter: Open unit in Lachine, and my first placement.

Le Village: Locked juvenile girls unit in St. Jerome, Quebec. This was a Ville Marie Social Services placement for clients waiting to go to Shawbridge Youth Center, The Farm. It wasn't on the Shawbridge campus (about 15 kms south), but it was referred to as a Shawbridge unit. On January 19, 1990, Michelle Thibault, Tina Poux, Christina Cain, and Tiffany Mackenzie died in a fire set by two other inmates. Due to a delay in locks springing open, they were unable to get out in time.
Le Village is also referred to in the book as simply, Village.

LSD: See Acid.

Montreal Forum: The former home of the Montreal Canadian NHL hockey team and a venue where concerts are held. It is located on the corner of Atwater and Ste. Catherine Street, across from the Montreal Children's Hospital.

Mrs. Beasley: A doll made by Mattel with a spotted blue dress and square eye glasses.

Ologists: Slang for any professional.

Out-of-body: The spirit leaving one's body due to extreme stress.

Slave to the Farm

Pavlovian boxes: Ivan Pavlov studied physiology and sciences. Pavlov is famous for the " conditioned reflex" concept. Pavlov learned that when a bell was rung while food was being presented to a dog over and over, the dog will salivate as the food is presented. The dog will later come to associate the ringing of the bell with the presentation of the food and salivate upon the ringing of the bell without the presentation of food.

Peak: When your high is at its highest.

Primary Worker: In each placement one of the staff members was assigned to each client. Your primary or sometimes just called your worker was in the unit with you and was like a "cottage parent".

Provi-Soire: A chain of convenience stores throughout Quebec. Also known as a depanneur.

Ride: A term used to describe someone's mode of transportation. It can apply to a car, motorcycle, bicycle, or in this case, dirt bike.

Room programs: Solitary confinement.

Session: When you smoke a round of spliffs.

Shawbridge Youth Centre: Influential Montreal businessmen started building the Shawbridge Boys

Slave to the Farm

Farm in 1908. It is a private institution. It was originally used as a training school for underprivileged, wayward, or orphaned boys. It was, and still is, a youth detention centre in the Laurentians mountains, 75 kms north of Montreal. Until the early 1990s it was an eight hundred acre farm with train tracks to the east and highway 117 to the west. Ville Marie Social Services, Shawbridge Youth Centre and a number of other Quebec Health and social services networks amalgamated into Batshaw Youth and Family Services in the early 1990s. At that time, 780 acres were sold off, leaving the original Farm sitting on 20 acres. In 1983-1986, while I was placed there, there were seven boys units/cottages: five open, two locked, I was in both of the girls units/cottages: one open and one locked. There were between ten and thirteen kids in each unit. We referred to it as 'The Farm'. See picture on inside front cover.

Skinner's box: B.F. Skinner was an American psychologist and behaviourist. Skinner invented the operant conditioning chamber also known as Skinner's Box in the late 1930s. Skinner's Box was used to study behaviour conditioning. When a subject performed correctly, the chamber mechanism delivered food or another reward. When a subject performed incorrectly, the mechanism delivered a punishment. For many years it was rumored that B.F. Skinner used his baby daughter Deborah in some of his experiments, and that she

259

committed suicide because of that trauma, but they have subsequently been proven untrue.

Smoking pit: Slang used to describe a designated smoking area.

Social Worker: A professional assigned to you by Ville Marie Social Services.

Spliff: Slang for a joint rolled with hash and tobacco usually containing no marijuana. See joint.

The Farm: See Shawbridge youth centre.

Tokes: Taking a haul, drag, pull, puff, hit, etc., on either a joint or a spliff.

Turning them out: To introduce someone to prostitution. Can also mean to live off the proceeds of someone else's prostitution.

Ville Marie Social Services: Ville Marie Social Services acted as the primary source of English clients to detention centres and Psychiatric hospitals in the Montreal area. A number of Quebec Health and Social Services networks including Ville Marie Social Services, Shawbridge Youth Centers, Youth Horizons, and others, were amalgamated in 1992. They are now Batshaw Youth and Family Centres.

Slave to the Farm

West Island: West of Dorval in Montreal is referred to as the West Island.

Youth Offenders Act: The *Juvenile Delinquents Act* was introduced in 1908. Those advocating for it promoted separate courts and detention centres for juveniles. The "best interest" of the child and more welfare type concern facilitated its passage. In 1984, the *Youth Offenders Act replaced the Juvenile Delinquents Act*. In 2003, the *Youth Criminal Justice Act* was introduced, replacing them both.

Youth Protection Act: The *Child Protection Act* (1944) was drawn up but not implemented. In 1950 the *Youth Protection Schools Act* redefined what industrial and reform schools were and established social welfare courts. Juvenile courts judges were given a broader mandate over placing welfare/protection cases into newly redefined "Youth-Protection Schools." These Youth-Protection Schools received a per diem in exchange for accepting the protection cases. Finally the *Youth Protection Act*, of 1977 was designed to keep all youth, including delinquents, from unnecessary contact with the courts. With the act came a newly created position of Director of Youth Protection for each social service centre. These directors were authorized with the dispositions of all troubled youth through the use of "voluntary measures". The courts were only used when a compulsory measure was necessary. The difference to some of us placed under protection in 1984-86 was that kids sentenced under the Youth Offenders Act for crimes they committed received a definite sentence, while Youth Protection cases, like myself, were given indefinite sentences. Shawbridge was instrumental in the early 1920s in lobbying for the indefinite sentencing of protection cases.

Acknowledgments

I have many people to thank. I'll start at home. I am so blessed to have my husband Will Pedlar, and our two beautiful daughters Rayana, and Olivia, inspiring me every day. (Thanks for the graphics, Rayana)

David Tafel, what can I say about a man who's loved me since before I was born? I couldn't be here without him. I love you Dad, and 'Thanks' isn't big enough!

Ellen Tolson, I owe you so much. She is my friend and neighbour, teacher, co-conspirator, editor, and muse. The sheet music at the start of each chapter is thanks to her endless talents. Xoxo.

My Mom and brothers, Jeff & Scott Tafel thanks for being there every step of the way.

Special thanks to Professor Eli Teram of Wilfrid Laurier University. Your generous support and efforts were instrumental in seeing me through.

I also want to thank Pru Rains and Frédéric Moisan for their faith in the project too.

Slave to the Farm

I thank the many Shawbridge Grads I've interviewed, Kris Tellier, Jason Fryer, Teena Clipston, Steve Scoffield, Dave Havey, Dave Wragg, Robert O'Connor, Daniel Bochner, Wendell James and so many many more. Azam, Leah, Marianne Moore-Souliere, Lee Reidl, Debbie Shaar, Tanja Michelle, Lorraine Dick, and so many more that should be on this list, thanks for everything.

And to all the people at Algonquin College who helped make this manuscript presentable I thank you from the bottom of my heart. Larry, thanks for walking us through the process.

About The Author

Erika Tafel lives in the Southern Okanagan of British Columbia with her husband and two daughters. They live off-grid using solar power and are in the process of building an underground home, which is the subject of her next book. She published a magazine, *The Wayward Dog*, and is a community activist with a strong belief in social justice issues.

For more information about Erika and this book, please visit: www.slavetothefarm.ca

Slave to the Farm